Ana Imagined

Ana Imagined

PERRIN IRELAND

Graywolf Press
Saint Paul, Minnesota

Publication of this volume is made possible in part by a grant
provided by the Minnesota State Arts Board through an
appropriation by the Minnesota State Legislature, and by a
grant from the National Endowment for the Arts. Significant
support has also been provided by the Bush Foundation;
Dayton's, Mervyn's, and Target stores through the Dayton
Hudson Foundation; the McKnight Foundation; and other
generous contributions from foundations, corporations, and
individuals. To these organizations and individuals we offer
our heartfelt thanks.

An excerpt from this novel was originally published in *AGNI* in
1999 in a slightly different form.

Published by Graywolf Press
2402 University Avenue, Suite 203
Saint Paul, Minnesota 55114
All rights reserved.

www.graywolfpress.org

Published in the United States of America

ISBN 1-55597-300-0

2 4 6 8 9 7 5 3 1
First Graywolf Printing, 2000

Library of Congress Catalog Card Number: 99-067241

Cover design: Julie Metz
Cover photograph: Gary Isaacs

Acknowledgments

Fiona McCrae and Anne Czarniecki gave life to this book; I will always be grateful. The entire Graywolf staff performed with extraordinary professionalism, energy, and kindness; I could not have asked for better collaborators. My thanks to Melinda Ward and Harriet Wasserman.

I am more grateful than I can say to Nela Hosic and Zehra Behremovic for reliving painful experiences in order to share information with me about life in Bosnia, and for reading this manuscript for factual accuracy. For details about Sarajevo, I relied on a number of sources, and am particularly indebted to the the following books and articles: *Letters from Sarajevo: Voices of a Besieged City* by Anna Cataldi; *Logavina Street: Life and Death in a Sarajevo Neighborhood* by Barbara Demick; *Portraits of Sarajevo* by Zlatko Dizdarevic (to whom I am indebted for his account of the true story of a child bringing food to his father, on which I drew for the anecdote on page 91); *Sarajevo: A War Journal* by Zlatko Dizdarevic; *The Balkan Express: Fragments from the Other Side of War* by Slavenka Drakulic; *Sarajevo Daily: A City and Its Newspaper Under Siege* by Tom Gjelten; *A Witness to Genocide* by Roy Gutman; *The Impossible Country: A Journey Through the Last Days of Yugoslavia* by Brian Hall; *Sarajevo, Exodus of a City* by Dzevad Karahasan (which included the definition of Sarajevo as "a resting place,"); *Love Thy Neighbor: A Story of War* by Peter Maass; *Yugoslavia: Death of a Nation* by Laura Silber and Allan Little; *Sarajevo Days, Sarajevo Nights* by Elma Softic; *Black Lamb and Grey Falcon: A Journey Through Yugoslavia* by Rebecca West; and "Surviving Sarajevo," by Elizabeth Rubin, in *Harper's Magazine*. The quotations from Anne Frank are from *Anne Frank: The Diary of a Young Girl.* The quotation from Rainer Maria Rilke is from *Letters to a Young Poet,* translated by M. D. Herter Norton.

I am deeply indebted to Amy Hempel, Jill McCorkle, Douglas Bauer, and, particularly, with respect to this book, Sheila Kohler, whose insightful reading of the manuscript was critical. My enduring gratitude to Liam Rector, Tree Swenson, and Askold Melnyczuk.

More friends than I can possibly mention have assisted me. I am particularly indebted to those who read early versions: Melinda Hurst, Cristina Del Sesto, Linda Feferman, Meredith Friedman, Wanda Pedas, Linda Podheiser, Susan Sonde, Ellen Steinbaum, Laura Welsh, and, with special thanks, Mirra Bank Brockman. My thanks to Sally Brady and her Tuesday morning writing group, The Good Luck Club, and to Sam Hurst.

I will always be deeply grateful to my parents and sisters, both for the constancy of their support, and for their example. To the Top Thirteen!

I thank Scott Ramey for his enthusiastic support.

My husband, Tom Ramey, read every word of every draft and dared to make invaluable suggestions. He never complained when I turned on the light in the middle of the night for an idea that couldn't wait, or when I shushed him in restaurants so I could listen to the conversation at the next table. He accompanied me to countless readings, lectures, and foreign films, none of them near sailboats. Mi corazón. Now I'll go to the grocery store.

To the people of the Balkans, I acknowledge the stupefying inadequacy of words.

Author's Note

This novel is a work of imagination, which, although fiction, strives for contextual accuracy. On rare occasions, for narrative purposes, I have altered details; in particular, I have placed the Sarajevo zoo in a location more accessible to Ana.

for Tom

and
Emma Randolph Hurst
Edward Hunter Hurst
Dorothy Bates Ramey

The truth doesn't care what we think of it.

Anne Michaels, *Fugitive Pieces*

Ana Imagined

At cocktail parties, people asked Anne why she was so interested in Bosnia.

She spoke eloquently and at length about the largest European holocaust since World War II. She discussed the West's early refusal to end the slaughter in spite of countless public refrains of "Never Again," the overwhelming historic significance of this development, and the absence of discussion about it. She rebutted the thesis of ethnic conflict, and offered intelligent, informed insight on global politics. She referenced morality and exhibited outrage.

She said nothing about what happened to her on February 14, 1970. Nothing about the terror of snow at midnight, the whoosh of a sliding glass door, the scent of blood on wool.

The ground was unforgiving. Ana pressed her foot down on the shovel and pushed, her breath like steam. She leaned her weight into it, feeling the wooden handle against her pelvic bone, the buttonless gray coat falling on either side. The frozen earth allowed for chipping, nothing more, and she scooped up crumbs and threw them behind her, adding the mixture of dirt and rock, not much larger than fingernail scrapings, to the small pile. The falling snow rested on her eyelashes and brushed against her bruised and swollen face, as she sank the blade into the ground again.

She felt eyes on her and whirled around.

❧

Anne stared at Ana's image on the television in her Cambridge, Massachusetts, apartment. She took a sip of lukewarm coffee from the mug with the Far Side cartoon on it, leaving a half ring of brown lipstick on the white ceramic, and placed the mug on the shelf with her Bosnia books.

She had no business writing about Ana.

The Secretary of State had said, "We don't have a dog in that fight."

Anne looked back at the television and studied the gash above Ana's left eye. She touched the thin, raised line on her own forehead.

She picked up her pen.

Sarajevo meant "resting place."

Beginning

1

Minarets, steeples, and domes soared heavenward from deep in the valley below, where orange-roofed white buildings basked along the river. Green hills lush with trees ringed the city.

Ana and Petar sat at the outdoor café perched on a hill dotted with apple and pear trees; white lilies grew in the adjoining garden. Ana's metal chair was unsteady, wobbly, and she pulled it closer to the rusted table. Not a shot had been fired.

The young girl at the stove dropped two spoonfuls of ground coffee into the copper dzezva, with its long, slender handle, then poured in boiling water. Clouds readied in the distance, the wind was from the east.

"There, they pour the water in first and then stir in the grounds," Petar said.

Ana tapped her foot, and looked at the Moorish building across the street.

The girl at the stove placed the copper pot on the fire, and, when it boiled, brought it over to Ana and Petar, pouring the Turkish coffee into small, handleless porcelain cups. A few coffee grounds floated to the surface.

Ana watched the steam rise, inhaled the pungent aroma, and sighed. She wrapped her fingers around the cup and sipped the thick, bitter coffee leisurely. While Petar gazed at the snow-blanketed peaks in the distance, she took a small flask from her purse and poured brandy into her cup, being careful not to spill, then returned the flask to the bag, stroking the black leather reassuringly; she didn't think he'd seen. She dipped her sugar cube in the coffee and sucked on it, and the sucking motion smeared brown lipstick from her lower lip onto her chin, which she wiped absentmindedly with her napkin. Ana thought about her son, Muhamed, who had fallen and cut his head the day before; she was anxious to see how it had healed.

Petar had been their neighbor for years, but had become increasingly irritating, a stone in the shoe. Ana's husband usually joined them, and she missed the buffer. Hairs grew out of Petar's ear, gray, not like the blond hair on his head. The flame on the stove rose higher.

"It doesn't make sense to pour the water in first," she said.

"If the water's already in the pot, the coffee grounds will seep into it the minute they're dropped in," he said.

"If the water's placed in the pot first, it will cool before the coffee grounds are added," she said.

"The water needs the moment to cool!" he said.

"It's barbaric!"

She knew she was being ridiculous, a train without brakes. She knocked her hand against her cup, tipping it over, and steaming coffee raced toward Petar's hand; she hoped he thought it was an accident.

He winced with pain as his fingers turned a fiery red, and shook his hand vigorously. Perhaps she'd gone too far.

Ana mopped up the spill with paper napkins, and studied the gold crescent and star at the bottom of the empty cup. Who cares how they make coffee in Serbia.

❧

It was raining when Ana left the café and stumbled on some rocks as she made her way to the car. She listened to the rain hitting the leaves and felt the water run off her hair onto her black leather jacket; she knew she should be concerned. She dropped her keys, dangling from a chain with a picture of birch trees on it, as she struggled to open the car door.

She turned the ignition, which didn't catch the first time, and waited, letting it rest as she looked out at the fog-enshrouded city below. A beautiful, peaceful city, sleeping by a river, snuggled in a valley. She would write a poem, the blinking lights as metaphor; she wrote her best poems when she'd been drinking. She'd publish the poem internationally, unwrapping her home for the world. People were shocked at how cosmopolitan Sarajevo was, and thought all Muslims wore veils and prayed five times a day. Ana's acquaintance with God was slight. She hadn't set foot in a mosque in twenty years; she'd gone with her Muslim mother. Her father was a Catholic Croat.

She tried again, the car started, and she turned on the windshield wipers; the left wiper made an annoying squeaking sound and smeared the grime on the windshield across her field of vision. She was out of windshield-wiper fluid. Ana was a car illiterate, frequently trying to get into parked cars that belonged to other people, thinking they were hers.

Leaning forward and straining to see, she started down the hill toward the center of town and turned on the car radio. Ana liked love songs, but didn't mention that to anyone as it clashed with her intellectual aspirations. She watched a soap opera, too, explaining to her husband that she was analyzing the writing style, the sociological content. Once someone had called her as part of a radio survey and asked what station she listened to and Ana had lied, identifying a news station. Now static interfered, she couldn't lose herself in the music, couldn't pretend to be younger, single.

Ana thought she saw Marko, Petar's eighteen-year-old cousin, walking alongside the road away from the city, although she wasn't sure. Whoever it was carried a beat-up, old, brown suitcase, string tied around it, and wore ill-fitting clothes and a cap pulled down low over his forehead. Marko worked on a farm in a small village near Sarajevo, and his grammar made her shudder. He'd come with Petar to the apartment yesterday, leaving a sliver of mud where his boot had been.

The pace of the rain increased dramatically, solid sheets

descending, dark, heavy clouds, like night, the enveloping fog thicker the closer she got to the heart of the city, and she pressed her foot down on the accelerator; Muhamed would be home from school soon. Here was the turn for her street already, no time to signal. The car jerked a hard right, and she braked, but the bald tires spun the car in a circle, out of control, and she watched helplessly as trees and houses whirled past.

So this is how it will be. If no other car is coming, I will live. If, by chance, another car comes, I will die.

❧

Ana pulled ten-year-old Muhamed down the street behind her on the way to the bookstore, looking back occasionally to check on him. He had his grandmother's dark eyes, and brown hair cut straight across his forehead, bowl-like, above long, up-curled lashes, and Ana loved the mono-chromatic look of his appearance—brown tones, sepia. She was interested in color juxtapositions—green trees against blue sky—and possessed a strong visual sense; once, before she could stop herself, she had held her hand up to her line of vision to block out the offending jowl of an other-wise beautiful woman. It calmed her, the aesthetic ordering. Her perfectionism left her in a chronic state of depression about her own appearance, although people frequently commented on her attractiveness.

She stumbled slightly when she turned to look at her reflection in a store window. Like other people, she pre-tended to be studying the window display.

Ana glanced across the street and was startled to see Petar sitting in the driver's seat of a car crammed full of luggage and belongings. When he saw that Ana had seen him, he turned away quickly and accelerated, disappearing.

What was that about? They never went on trips without informing each other; nothing had happened between them to incite that kind of behavior. Years ago, before she married, she and Petar had had an affair, although her husband didn't know. There was no need. There was something more important from the past that she'd kept from Emir.

She walked past the block-long Holiday Inn, a twelve-story yellow box across from the Parliament building, and the adjacent park. "How odd," Muhamed was saying. Muhamed was always saying things like "how odd" or "regrettably" or "unconscionable"—words that sounded peculiar coming out of his ten-year-old mouth, and Ana sometimes imagined him with a bow tie, umbrella, and bowler hat. He absorbed his environment in its entirety, indiscriminately, processed it objectively, scientifically, before emitting precise bits of conclusive data.

"How odd," he said again, and Ana followed his gaze to large splotches of dried blood on the sidewalk. A black hand-painted protest sign had been flung into the bushes lining the bloodied walkway, and people had placed flowers—roses, marigolds, white violets—around the brown spills.

She pulled Muhamed closer and picked up speed, practically dragging him. Occasionally his feet flew into the air, brown laces flapping, when he didn't place them on the ground fast enough. His head was still twisted behind him as he stared at the stained sidewalk. She read the buildings around her, the signs and plaques, and on impulse, turned into Zijo's.

"Muhamed!" Zijo said. Muhamed glowered.

While Muhamed held his ground near the door, Ana walked up and down the aisles of the small, dusty store, eyeing the shapes and colors, past bananas and cigarettes, German beer. Tangerines, and Toblerone chocolate bars. People moved too slowly, and she pushed around them. She made her selection, and Zijo placed it in a brown paper bag. She knew none of the other customers.

Muhamed preceded her out of the store, nearly running, and they moved silently back down the street on which they'd come. When they arrived at the blood-splattered sidewalk, they stopped. The street was almost empty, and Ana stooped, knees cracking, and set the bag down carefully beside her on the concrete. She picked the flowers and petals up gently, admiring the fragility of the violets, the marigolds' depth of color, and laid them to the side, then opened her purse, and removed a package of moist towelettes. She tore open the tinfoil seal and unfolded one of the wipes, which she used to scrub at the bloodstains. The wet cloth held a bitter, lemon smell, antiseptic. Birds were singing, soon roses would bloom. She was experiencing a relieving sense of peace and stopped scrubbing long enough to hand Muhamed a towelette, and he, too, stooped down and wiped at the blood. Watching her out of the corner of his eye, he shifted position, forcefully kicking the brown paper bag with the bottle, which crashed and broke, sending a river, then streams, of vodka running down the sidewalk.

❧

Days later, when the first shells hit, the whole building shook with deafening sound, and Ana gripped the dresser to steady herself with her left hand, held her glass with the right. She waited for the rumbling to subside, then looked out the window at the mosque, the northeast corner of which had evaporated, thick, black smoke pluming skyward. It was not possible.

It was one of the pretty, rose-colored wineglasses that had belonged to her aunt, smaller than the ones manufactured these days, and although the red wine was not quite the same shade as the goblet, it worked somehow.

The bedroom was spartan and neat, and besides the antique dresser that had belonged to her mother, only a bed and chair sat on the highly polished hardwood floor, a pink and gray oriental rug centered between the bed and dresser. Ana didn't like to be surrounded by too many objects; they were oppressive, things screaming to be fixed and cleaned. On the white walls, she'd hung a large, rose-colored abstract painting in which the outline of a nude female was barely discernible, a brown-ink drawing of a man dancing, and a framed strip of blue, hand-embroidered Chinese silk populated with pagodas and men pulling rickshaws.

Muhamed sprawled on the rug playing with a wooden

horse. He followed her from room to room, which pleased her enormously; just looking at him could make her quiver. Sometimes she thought her love for him was too strong, symbiotic; her own mother had been harsh, and Ana knew she overcompensated with Muhamed. To comfort is to be comforted, she'd read. Muhamed galloped the horse this way and that, making clucking noises and whinnies as the horse leapt and pirouetted.

Emir, Ana's husband, entered in stocking feet and examined the curtainless window frame, tracing a hairline fracture traveling along the east wall. "We need a carpenter." Emir, a playwright, was writing a rock opera based on the life of Anne Frank.

He picked up the horse from Muhamed, raised it high in the air, and danced around the room, dipping the horse up and down as if it were an airplane. Both Ana and Emir had developed slight potbellies, which they pretended not to notice in the other. Muhamed jumped up and grabbed his father around his stocky legs, like a bear cub hugging a tree. She could usually watch them play for hours, but not tonight.

Ana put on her silver, crescent-shaped earrings. She and Mira were going to their poetry group, continuing to attend the meetings at the home of the renowned poet in spite of the fact that the woman had named her cats Truth and Beauty. Thank God Mira was back from Zagreb; Ana had missed the sounds of chairs moving in the apartment above, the bed creaking. Petar hadn't returned since the day of the protest, the day she and Muhamed had tried to wash the blood away, and his fourth-floor apartment lay empty.

"We're meeting at Luben's," she said to Emir.

"Vasa Miskin Street should be okay," he said.

He examined the crack in the wall. "A carpenter."

❧

Ana fingered the pillowcases at Luben's Linens. She selected white, with a delicate lace border, and paid a woman whose face was too long. She and Mira were the only customers; Mira hadn't wanted to come at all.

"Let's stop for a drink," she said to Mira on their way out of the building.

"She'll give us something there."

"I need something to get me there."

"Don't read anything if you don't want to."

The two women stopped and held onto each other as an ear-shattering blast split the air. Ana tried to block out the sound, imagining a triumphant burst of trumpets. The West would never tolerate an assault on Sarajevo.

When the ground ceased trembling, the women continued.

They produced sudden smiles when Vera opened the door of her antique-laden apartment, her white hair swept up behind her with tortoiseshell combs, a nice contrast with her pink sweater. The poet's residence was filled with warm, soft colors and designs, overlaid with incense, and what sounded like wind chimes; one had the sense of a hearth, although there was none. A painting of the bridge at Mostar—a surprisingly conventional touch—hung above a bookshelf.

18

Ana and Mira, both wearing black, took their seats in the living room with the others. Aaron nodded curtly and continued reading the article he grasped, while curly-haired Melina smiled incessantly and attempted to draw Nedjo into conversation. Nedjo was interested, but holding all the cards. Ana pretended to be fond of the cat that had strolled over and rubbed up against her leg, but the cat was uninterested in Ana's attempts to chuck it under the chin, and wandered off.

A loud boom sounded in the distance like a thunderous drumroll. Ana tried to think about alliteration.

"Coffee?" Vera offered. No brandy.

"Did you hear about Bosa?" Melina asked.

They clucked over the former group member's latest misfortune.

"Shall we?" Vera said. She put on her glasses. "I thought we might begin with a brief reading from Rilke." She peered over her glasses at them, smiling. "If you'll permit me."

"Oh, please!" Melina said. The others nodded. Ana rolled her eyes at Mira.

Vera began: "'Therefore, dear sir, love your solitude and bear with sweet-sounding lamentation the suffering it causes you. For those who are near you are far, you say, and that shows it is beginning to grow wide about you. And when what is near you is far, then your distance is already among the stars and very large.'"

Ana was moved in spite of herself, but when she saw the look of rapture on Vera's face, the tears in her eyes, Ana's own emotion dissipated in a cloud of self-rebuke. Sentimental fool.

Vera quietly, gently, closed the book, placed it on the coffee table, and maintained a meditative silence for a full moment, which no one dared disturb.

"Now then," she said, looking up. "Who would like to begin?" She looked at Aaron, who brought copies of his poem out of his briefcase and passed them around.

Ana read it quickly. She admired his work, which was intelligent, informed, dark. She didn't always understand it, and enjoyed the not understanding.

He read in a deep, resonant voice. When he finished, there was silence.

Nedjo spoke first. "What did you mean in the next-to-the-last line?"

"Yogurt as technology."

"Ah." Everyone nodded, strained to grasp it.

"I thought parachutes were always white," Melina offered. "Isn't it a safety issue?" She looked at Nedjo for approval.

"I liked 'ruby riot,'" Ana said.

Suddenly the building shook and they grabbed their chairs, sitting very still, as the wind chimes clanged erratically. Ana tried to remember the quality of the bark on a birch tree she admired. She thought about the shine of Muhamed's eyes. The Americans were surely on their way to help.

Vera looked at her watch. "Ana?"

The breath was knocked out of her, and she felt the blood rush to her face. Her hands began to shake as she carefully opened her folder, trying to appear calm and to keep the pages from flying about. She took out the copies of her poem and passed them around.

She was cheating. It was a poem she'd written fifteen years ago, which she'd pulled from a pile based on one criterion—it was the shortest poem she'd ever written. Humorous, she thought. She and Emir always read each other's work, and he seemed to like it.

She cleared her throat, read.

Afterward, she saw Aaron smile to himself; good, no one else mattered. Mira read it thoughtfully, as if she'd never seen it.

A roar surged through the room like a tidal wave; the building shook, coffee cups rattled.

"Bones," Vera said. "Flesh it out, slow it down." She looked at her watch again. "Melina, do you have something?"

Melina could hardly wait and quickly pulled out copies of her poem and distributed them. She read.

Ana couldn't believe what she was hearing. Melina was describing a sexual encounter, and it was clear that it was with Nedjo; she had described him perfectly. How could she be so dense as to think they wouldn't know?

When Melina had finished reading, she looked up expectantly. Nedjo looked furious, but didn't say anything. Ana stared at her feet.

"What energy!" Mira said.

Melina beamed.

Silence.

"That's . . . a point of view," Aaron offered.

"Red cradle toy!" Nedjo shouted. "You stole my image!"

"I did not!" Melina said. "How would I know you had a red cradle toy?"

"From my poem, you dimwit! The one I read here last month!" He was standing, shaking.

Melina burst into tears. "I would *never* steal from you! You haven't written an interesting poem in months! Who *gives* a fuck what your breakfast reminds you of?"

Ana and Mira exchanged glances; this was too good to be true.

Nedjo started toward Melina, who stood, while Vera gasped and put a hand at her throat, and Ana and Mira jumped up. Aaron held Nedjo by the arm.

"What the hell do *you* know!" Nedjo turned to Aaron. "About *life*?!"

Aaron looked perplexed, searched for a way to catalog the events, speak about them rationally.

"Let's try to think how Rilke would handle this," Vera said. "Remember how he said learn to love the questions themselves?"

Nedjo thundered out of the apartment, Melina locked herself in the bathroom, Aaron returned the coffee cups to the kitchen.

❧

Ana and Mira collapsed on Ana's sofa laughing. Ana ran out of the room and returned with a white sheet, which she wrapped around herself, before sitting down cross-legged on the floor. "Who am I?"

Mira shook her head.

"Rilke Gandhi."

It was uproarious.

Ana picked up the rose wineglass and sipped, looking out the window into the night at the dark hole where the mosque used to be. Like a mouth's missing tooth.

∽

"Your temper," Emir said the next morning, lying beside her in bed. Ana had asked him to name her fatal flaw, a diverting game, she'd thought, like what do you want for an epitaph? Emir wanted to be remembered as an interesting person, while Ana wanted something about having done good in the world; she would work on the wording. Last week she'd seen a Rodin sculpture at the museum, so stunning it slapped her. If I could write a poem that beautiful, my life would not have been in vain.

She was irritated at Emir's suggestion that she had a temper. "Hmm," she said. "Possibly." She ran her finger across the soft valley in the pillow.

Out the window, her favorite birch tree stood guard; three trunks grew out of the earth and spread delicate limbs, black eyes burnt onto the white bark. Black on white, she loved the drama of it.

She turned and studied the effect of their blue-gray bedroom wall against the white molding. Nice.

She looked at Emir. The air around him was charged; the most banal conversation became wildly erotic. She admired the fullness of his black hair and beard; her own dark hair hung straight and limp down her back. Although her blue eyes were as vibrant as his, she believed. A little too close together. Hers, not his. "What?" she said.

"Otto Frank. When he was interviewed after it was over, he referred to himself as a German."

"Did you know there was cannibalism in the camps? Mira told me."

He turned to face her. "Well?"

She stared at the ceiling. "What do *you* think?"

"That's not what I asked."

"Here's the deal," Emir said finally. "If *you* want more children, *I* want more children."

❦

Here's the deal? What self-respecting Bosnian would say such a thing? Anne scratched it out.

❦

Ana traced the curve of his ear, like a seashell, with her tongue.

Emir moved beneath her and rolled her over on her back. He started kissing her tentatively on the throat, his full lips brushing against her skin. Behind her ear. Ana touched his smooth skin, taut, like a ball pumped full of air, a thick-stalked mushroom. She wrapped her mouth around it, bathing, her long black hair falling about them like a tent. She brought him to her. She moved her hips, and the mattress gave way and sank, up and down, but not too much, up and down the moist walls. He grabbed the headboard, held and pulled, faster and harder. They rolled over, she sat up, more slowly now.

She leaned forward, nipples barely brushing against his chest, and felt the sun from the window, the sweat between her breasts. He sat up, hugging her to him, closer, as close as possible, her bare arms and legs wrapped around him.

Startled, Ana opened her eyes as shattered glass fell from the window to the bed; there was a hole in the white bedsheet. She leaned around Emir, reached, slid her finger through, plucking out a sniper's bullet where Emir's chest had been.

She imagined blood red against white.

❦

Anne wondered if anyone would misunderstand and think Emir had actually been shot. Maybe she should rephrase the last paragraph.

Anne's father had been shot in the head during World War II, and now he had Alzheimer's. "I love you more than I know," he'd told her.

Her attempts to remember what her father had been like before were not fruitful; her husband accused her of auto-biographical amnesia. A plague of forgetting.

Anne had been raised in Montgomery, Alabama, and wore gloves and hats to the local Episcopal church, where she positioned herself in a beatific pose and drank in drama. She was confirmed in a white, empire-style sheath dress, very sophisticated, and remembered nothing else of the service. Her brothers looked after her and, in general, followed the rules, requiring her to seek definition elsewhere. She tied tacky orange scarves around the necks of her school dresses in a tepid challenge to the oppression of good taste, and dressed as a gypsy every Halloween, wallowing in large, dime-store hoop earrings.

She was taught to curtsy and didn't have to open doors. She had a nanny who cried when she smiled, tears leaking from the inner corner of her left eye. She and her friends wrote and performed plays as children; she was always the princess.

She walked in her sleep and had vivid, hallucinatory dreams, but didn't want to disturb her parents when she had nightmares—her mother was anxious and her father dis-tracted—and would spend the rest of the night sitting in the hall at the top of the stairs. She didn't want to burden her *parents with secrets, either, and told them nothing, not even about the wolf in the closet. For a year she didn't speak, and was towed to a variety of doctors who found nothing wrong.*

Her mother had loved to read, after she'd bathed, dressed, and perfumed for dinner. She finished every book saying, "Of course, I've never known anyone like that." They knew only the best sorts of people. Anne's thirteenth great-grandmother was Pocahontas (an exception to Virginia's laws against miscegenation was made for the descendants of Pocahontas), and her mother was a member of the DAR, only you weren't supposed to tell because probably whomever you told was ineligible.

Reading was permitted after Anne slept during naptime (she understood that the purpose of naptime was to free her mother), but Anne cheated, skipped the sleeping part, and went straight to the reading part. This was her only lie, about the sleeping. Lying troubled Anne and her family a great deal, as did any kind of bad behavior. They believed in clothes laid out the night before, cod liver oil every morning.

When Anne had an appendectomy, she tried to stay awake during the operation so she could thank the doctor. She read a New Yorker *cartoon labeled "Self-Esteem." It was a picture of a man writing in his diary: "Dear Diary, I'm sorry to be bothering you again."*

Anne had wanted very much to be good and was determined to read the Bible straight through from cover to cover; her Bible had a soft, red leather cover with her name on it in gold lettering, and thin, white pages edged with gold. She read the first few pages of Genesis thirty-three times. Now she raged at God; she had been for twenty-five years.

Anne's father and brothers never raised their voices or cursed in front of her; gentlemen didn't. They would take care of anything difficult or disturbing, as it was best not to mention these things to the ladies. Otherwise, she might have been better prepared.

Middle

2

Emir Gusic
Sarajevo

Dear Mr. Gusic:

I am in receipt of your three letters requesting assistance with the matter of the attacks on Sarajevo.

I want to assure you that we have the greatest respect for the awkwardness of your situation; we bear daily witness to graphic television footage, which is afforded the most careful attention and interest.

There are a number of factors, however, which render the use of American forces problematic. For example, we're told that ethnic conflict has characterized the region for generations, and that it would be difficult, in fact impossible, to put a dent in such a tradition. And, with all respect, I feel I must mention that the recent unpleasantness in Rwanda, the hacking and chopping, is more significant, I believe, in numerical terms (I cannot be certain, as we are provided little information, and very few pictures, of that more alien conflict. Perhaps they have been killing each other for centuries, also, and, in any case, who knows what goes on in the minds of such people?)

But I bring up Rwanda simply to remind you, unnecessarily, that misunderstandings span the globe, and I know you can appreciate the sad truth that we cannot, regrettably, police them all. Look at Somalia. Indians are being killed in Guatemala. And nuns, I believe, in El Salvador. You see where I'm going. Therefore, it is with deep regret, and sincere good wishes, that we must reject your appeal. As you requested, I'm sending this letter to your post office box.

Sincerely,
Walker Highsmith
Yugoslavia Desk
Department of State
Washington, D.C.
USA

P.S. I wonder if you would be so kind as to sign my copy of your magnificent play, "Death of the Lily," enclosed. It's such a pleasure to be in contact with an artist of your stature.

"I'm expecting a letter," Emir said.

Ana turned in bed and looked over at him. Mail wasn't getting through. Weeks had passed since she first saw blood on the sidewalk, since the first shells hit, and the denial of those early days had given way to a grinding stupor as they lurched incredulously through the nightmare, all of Ana's desires concentrated on bringing Muhamed safely through the war.

The sounds of morning—Serb sniper fire, machine-gun blasts, explosions echoing through the hills—filled the room. They had covered the window with plywood to keep out bullets, and Emir had painted a moon and stars on the wood; when they got up, he would replace the moon and stars with a bright orange sun. Ana's stomach was permanently clenched. When she awoke, she had the few seconds before she remembered. Sometimes a shot preceded the thought.

"It should have arrived by now," Emir said.

Ana rose and moved through the shades of gray to her desk, where her long, faded pink nightgown fell around her feet as she sat. She pushed her hair behind small ears, felt for matches, and lit the candle. The flickering flame drew her in, and she lost herself in its pull for a moment before shaking herself free.

She put her finger in the flame, withdrew it, and glanced at the silver-framed picture of her mother as a smiling young woman. Everyone told her how much her mother had laughed before she married. Red had been her mother's favorite color, and the day after her mother died, a redbird appeared at Ana's window, tapping, tapping, returning every day that month to provide comfort.

The side of the wooden drawer caught briefly as Ana slid it out from the desk and removed a spiral notebook and pen. She'd begun writing a poem, for Muhamed, first thing every morning, before the dream dissolved. She wrote about her childhood in Sarajevo, she wrote with obsession. Today it was a barefoot picnic by the river, under a plum tree, a bright sunny day. A long swim after the food had been digested, the swiftly moving clouds, the goose-bump chill of the wind, the bee sting.

More and more, Ana was tempted to tell Emir her secret. For the first time in years, she felt it required action. She remembered cries.

∞

Ana entered Muhamed's room; his bed was pulled far from the window, almost to the door. He was wide awake.

"Is it precisely 5:30 A.M.?" he asked.

"Approximately precisely." She heard Emir playing the piano, singing, and wished that she could sing. She would like that better than writing, music partook of the soul.

"Dreams?" she asked Muhamed.

"I've told you. Nothing alarming." He raised his hand to her cheek and stroked it.

"What would you like for breakfast?" she asked.

"Rice."

They ate rice every morning. Macaroni for lunch,

boiled rice and bread for dinner. Occasionally soybeans. There were days they revelled in spontaneity and had macaroni for dinner and rice for lunch.

Emir sat at the table building a structure out of rice cakes. "Shall we give it a tower?" he asked Muhamed. A collection of tiny porcelain coffee cups sat in the china cupboard behind him.

"A minaret," Muhamed said. "I forget, how many balconies did it have?" Only two months had passed since the mosque was shelled. Muhamed hadn't questioned the city's devastation. It was as if he'd expected it and simply followed his parents with his eyes, alert for breakage.

"As many balconies as you want." Emir thumped his middle finger against his forehead. "As many as you want."

Ana poured them each a half glass of water, finishing the canister. Muhamed was always thirsty. Tea for her and Emir.

"I should like to be a mathematician," Muhamed said.

"And a fine mathematician you'd be, too," Ana said, her heart breaking a little at the dullness of it. "What are you going to read this morning?" She didn't hear his response as she watched Emir, who was moving rice around his plate, not eating.

"Is your class still meeting this afternoon?" she asked Emir. A handful of his playwrighting graduate students met in the cellar of the university administration building.

"Much Ado About Nothing."

It was July, hot. Ana pulled the sweater off of the back of her chair and put it on.

❦

"Too fragile," Ana said to Emir, as she bent to the ground. "You've made her too fragile."

"Protected," he said. His collarbone stuck out sharply through his shirt.

Clumps of dirt caught in her fingernails as Ana picked up twigs. "How protected could she have been once they moved to the annex? A star pinned to her jacket."

"She didn't want to think about it." His eyes darted across the hills from time to time.

Ana vacillated between thinking Emir was a genius and fearing for his sanity. It interested her that people could be so smart in one category, so dumb in another.

Emir rearranged the brown branches in his left arm, reached to the ground with his right. He had located an old wood-burning stove somewhere and dragged it back to the apartment. She admired his initiative; if they were being bombed back to the Stone Age, he was turning out to be a good caveman. She thought about her role, about Muhamed, about the secret. She remembered how the pain had suddenly ceased, she'd been flushed with warmth.

There were more families collecting wood in the park on Djuro Djakovic Street than Ana had seen there before, and she felt her adrenaline pumping, a sense of competition that shamed her. It was for Muhamed, she reminded herself. She rose and stretched, resting her back before shifting the sticks to ease the itch on her arm, but now she had a poke and had to reorganize again, to stabilize, so she could add more.

She looked around the park, and remembered when it was foliage filled, with children playing tag on the grass, wooden benches for the old people; she and Muhamed had rested on the far knoll. The benches had been among the first items snatched for firewood. Silver birches, fir and plum trees, even a magnolia tree, had leaned and whispered above the green. Chestnut, oak, and tall spruce, powdered white in winter. Lilacs. She didn't wonder when, if, the park would look that way again, didn't allow such thoughts.

Ana and Emir froze as they heard the crackle of Serb gunshots emerging from the hills above the city. They didn't seem to be coming close.

"When does the next music come?" she asked, bending down again, being careful with her back.

"The next scene. A Nazi chorus."

Ana dropped her pile of wood, which clattered to the ground, a couple of twigs bouncing into the air as she gaped. She stared across the park and let loose with a series of spine-tingling screams, running toward a man chopping a green branch off of a tree with an ax. *Not the live ones!*

The balding, middle-aged man looked at her blankly, then resumed chopping.

Ana could feel the tree bleeding. She slipped on some pebbles and almost fell, but regained her footing and charged the man, throwing her arms around his legs, knocking him off balance, sending them both tumbling.

Emir was right behind and pounced, pulling her off her victim.

❦

The birch tree outside her window was gone. Ana returned to her poetry book, tried to focus. She would leave early in the morning for the water line; Muhamed was always thirsty.

She looked at the wood-burning stove centered in the living room. A painting she cherished hung on the far wall—a woman's face emerging eerily from a smokey background. The woman wore an extraordinary but indecipherable expression. Ana had spent great lengths of time studying her and had concluded that she was strong and sad, but not *sad* sad, because of the strength. She would not allow others to pity her, would be contemptuous of them for it. She was all knowing, incapable of being surprised. She persevered. She was without joy. But, also, without bitterness, anger.

Emir played the piano with gusto, pounding it mercilessly against the day they would use it for firewood.

❦

It grew dark.

Ana and Emir were attending Mira's photography exhibit at the gallery; everyone had to bring his own candle. Nisveta, from the apartment down the hall, was looking after Muhamed, and Ana had instructed her to take him to the basement if the shelling began.

Ana approached Mira's first black-and-white photograph, a picture of a kitten, and had a sinking sensation.

The next one was of a smiling child sitting on a stoop with a flowerpot. Oh God, not even an oblique angle. Maybe that was the point, maybe Mira was commenting on banality in the midst of chaos; Ana felt a thrill at her friend's brilliance. Although it would be a risky opinion to venture. The men and women around her were studying the photographs intently, looking a little shabbier than they used to, thinner. More of the men had beards, more of the shirts had stains. Nothing was ironed.

A man pointed out a photograph to his companion, and Ana snuck up behind them trying to see what he saw. She never knew how close to stand to an object in a gallery; she preferred to see it from both close and far, but the pleasure of the close view was marred by her anxiety that she was blocking the view of someone behind her. Candlelight complicated. She was tired and longed for a bench.

She became increasingly apprehensive about seeing Mira, who was being greeted by well-wishers in the far corner. Emir was inspecting the photographs carefully. He would be kind; he adored Mira, and she him. Ana occasionally, casually, pointed out Mira's shortcomings to Emir. Very offhandedly. Last week she'd drawn attention to Mira's thinning hair.

Emir came up behind Ana and poked a finger in her back like a gun.

"She could have used pastels," he said.

"Or included puppies."

"Let her be."

"I don't want to lie."

"Ask a question. People never notice you haven't rendered judgment."

All the times he had asked her questions about her writing flew through her mind.

"I want to support her," she said.

"Carry her camera."

"What are you going to say?" she asked.

"That I like kittens."

"You hate kittens."

"It's cats I hate. She has persuaded me that I love kittens. We must get one immediately."

Ana turned away.

Emir walked over to an acquaintance and inquired about the mail situation.

The more compelling photographs were probably coming up. Mira had no doubt saved the strongest for the finish, a good strategy. Ana experienced a rising panic—it climbed up into and constricted her throat—as she viewed the remaining works and practically bumped into Mira, who was standing just past the last photograph.

"I'm so *excited* for you!" Ana said, throwing her arms around Mira. She thrust the flowers she had brought into Mira's face, buying several seconds.

∞

On the way home in the dark, Ana and Emir walked past a pack of mangy dogs rooting through heaps of uncollected garbage. A boy with one leg leaned against a smoke-blackened building punctured by shrapnel. Had he been in Muhamed's class? Weeds grew in the rubble where the mosque had been.

"We need to talk about classical music," Emir said.

He needed a haircut.

"In the camps, Otto Frank survived by talking about things like Beethoven's Ninth."

"Couldn't we talk about books?"

"Classical music."

❧

Emir stopped licking when a shell exploded not far from the building.

The blood throbbed in Ana's swollen genitals like a heartbeat; her womb ached, her body arched.

Emir got up and walked over to the window, peering out through a crack in the boards, checking for fire.

Ana lay still, waiting for the pulsing to subside.

Emir returned to bed. "Let's remember when we met."

"Why?"

"It was delicious."

"You came over to the table to talk with Mira."

"I was overwhelmed by your charm."

"I said nothing."

"That was it. Your sullen beauty. Bespeaking depths of passion."

"Bespeaking paralyzing timidity."

"You were always thinking. I loved that."

"Brooding."

"The timidity is gone."

"Do you miss it?"

"It would have bored me after I became accustomed to your beauty."

"What bores you now?"

"That you're always thinking."

I wonder if he means while we're talking or when I'm quiet. He could mean thinking in the middle of the night, is it the amount of time spent thinking, the quality of the thinking . . .

"Where did Muhamed come from?" he said.

"A mourning dove dropped him at our doorstep."

"I think he's one of the tsar's lost children."

"He's perfect."

"Yes."

❧

Eric, Anne's teenaged son, was still asleep, and she suppressed the first stirrings of tension she felt on weekend mornings when he was not up making calls about summer jobs.

She fondled the first few pages of her novel about Ana. She planned to immerse herself in the Bosnian nightmare, square off with evil, tame it.

The depth of her passion for the task surprised even her. She didn't regard it as personal, as relating to the events of February 14, 1970, but had a long tradition of separating her conscious thoughts from the deepest reverberations of her psyche.

Her dog, Margaret, rose up on her hind legs on the polished, hardwood floor, threw her head back, and howled. Anne walked into the foyer, pushed Margaret's nose away from the mail slot, and picked up the letter from the man who'd taught her fiction class.

Dear Anne:

Your novel about Ana sounds intriguing, and ambitious. Since you ask, I do have some thoughts. While I understand, and respect, your concern about Bosnia, and your desire to write about it, I wonder if you're not biting off more than you need. The act of writing alone is difficult enough without adding the significant burden of setting it in an unfamiliar landscape. From where will you obtain the small details so essential to good fiction? What about authority? How will you compete with the multitude of books that will surely pour out of the Bosnian wound, books written by people who have lived it? Is it necessary to use Bosnia?

*In short, what you propose is extremely difficult,
and, while you'll have to make up your own mind . . .*

*Anne carefully folded the letter in half and placed it in the
dictionary under teacher. She closed the large book and
pressed down, leaning all of her weight on it.*

3

Ana positioned Muhamed as far away from the living-room window as possible the next morning, and supplied him with crayons and paper along with his books. He had learned to recognize the hiss of an incoming artillery shell and move before it hit.

She brushed rice from his cheek and stood back and gazed at his pasty complexion. "Think what you might want for lunch."

After surveying the street from behind the partially opened door, Ana and Mira left the apartment building, pulling Muhamed's rusty red wagon, with its cargo of empty water canisters, behind them. The wagon had a bullet nick above the left rear tire and squeaked as it rolled along. Potholes tore into streets littered with shattered glass and rubble, and small birds hopped around on exploded, colored bits of furniture and toys mixed in with pieces of concrete and wood from demolished buildings.

Ana's tongue was thick cotton.

I live in a slum. She thought about Mevla Omerovic, a girl from school who'd lived in a poor neighborhood, a girl she hadn't thought about in years. Why was it that people expected life would get better and better, like a happy ending to a novel? It was this expectation that made going backward so painful, the endless losses. If they'd been born into horror, wouldn't it have been easier?

Ana and Mira walked briskly through streets absent of cars, except those destroyed and abandoned; Ana and Emir's had been shelled the second week of the siege. People traveled by foot, for the most part, or on bicycles with baskets for provisions.

A variety of imaginatively constructed carts—plywood on roller skates, wheels lashed to chairs, upside-down tables, reconstructed skateboards, etc.—were used to transport possessions. Those piled high with clothes, pots, and pans belonged to the residents whose apartments had been destroyed overnight, people on their way to new dwellings. Flames shot out of buildings like torches. Ana had a pale, rice-paper memory of majestic, tree-lined avenues packed with cheering crowds waving colorful flags during the 1984 Olympics.

A couple of turbaned mujahideen walked by, and Ana frowned at the foreigners, fanatics who treated their women horribly.

Fire had blackened the buildings, some fortified with concrete slabs, all pockmarked by shells. Birds nested in the holes in the walls. Occasionally a rocket whistled over-head; Ana had been told that you never hear the bullet that kills you.

Ana and Mira arrived at Sniper Alley, between Djuro Djakovic Street and Marsala Tita, where the dark, asphalt road was pitted with craters, like an acned face; streetlights had been shot out and dangled from wires, and trolley cars were tipped over to shield pedestrians. A 100-square-foot area was exposed to snipers hidden in the bombed-out, white twin apartment towers of the Grbavica suburb, twenty-five yards away, at the north end of the boulevard. Grbavica connected to Sarajevo at the Bridge of Brother-hood and Unity.

Ana's breath was brisk. A white, UN armored person-nel carrier accompanied pedestrians attempting to cross, and Mira went first, crouching beside the carrier, running as it rolled along, her brown dress jerking with the effort. When Mira reached the other side she turned and waved, and the vehicle returned to Ana's side.

Ana's jaw tightened as she leaned close to the tank and ran for her life, pulling a child's red wagon squeaking behind her. When she arrived at the other side, she straight-ened and grinned at the bank of television cameramen awaiting a fatality. She thrilled at their disappointment, the curtailment of their careers.

A red-haired cameraman wearing a T-shirt with the logo of an American television network trained his camera on her anyway.

She felt giddy as she and Mira proceeded to the next intersection, where they paused with other pedestrians huddled against a building, everyone looking up at the sniper-infested hills, awaiting some instinct to tell them it was safe to cross. A brief hesitation, then Ana and Mira scurried across and formed the end of the water line, which usually involved a two- or three-hour wait. Emir was in the bread line; all the bread would be gone by eight.

Ana stared at the back of the head of the woman in front of her and the contrast between the half of her hair that was bleached blond and the several inches of black hair growing from the roots. The root line was a sort of time line, Ana realized, measuring the distance from an era in which one could access beauty supplies and the time and interest they required. A young man behind them hugged a radio playing Elton John.

She'd seen a nature film once on television—a desert during a drought. One water hole remained, where all the animals gathered to drink, but it was teeming with croco-diles, and, one by one, the animals who came to drink were eaten. At first the baboons had tried to rescue other baboons, but later, none of them bothered.

"Van Gogh," Ana said. It was a game she and Mira played—what if you had to live in a world populated with the paintings of a single artist?

"Good, but not always calming," Mira said. "Monet?"

"Not the water lilies."

"Did you hear about the Bosnian man digging the trench?" someone ahead of them in line called out.

"He kept digging this trench. Finally someone said to him, why are you still digging? The trench is already eight feet deep. And the man said, if I find oil, the Americans will come."

"El Greco," Ana said.

"Renoir."

"Maybe if we were whales, someone would stop the slaughter," someone said.

"Modigliani." If she weren't Sarajevan, she'd like to be Italian.

"Let's come to the aid of Europeans," a man said.

"It's hopeless," another man said. "Europeans are mired in ethnic conflict—the English, French, and Germans have been fighting each other for centuries."

Picasso.

A sniper struck. The crack of the shot, the zip of the bullet, the echo. Again. Silence. A man and woman leaving the building with their water dropped to the ground.

People screamed and dashed for cover; Ana and Mira sprinted to the building, stooped, and pressed against its walls. The murdered couple lay still, in ever-widening pools of blood; the wife's left arm flopped over her husband's body. Their young daughter started pulling on them, screaming. Pulling, pulling the dead bodies, shrieking.

Who would get their water.

Pulling and screaming. Children need their mothers.

Ana and Emir tried not to go anyplace together anymore.

She'd heard Serbs got 500 deutsche marks a head, that they practiced slitting people's throats by cutting pig throats. She needed to go to the bathroom.

The young girl's howls continued, everyone else was silent.

A woman crossed herself with two fingers, a Catholic Croat. A man crossed himself with two fingers and a thumb, an Orthodox Serb.

❧

The electricity had come on for a few hours; Muhamed watched Serb cartoons on television while Emir read, looked up at the screen from time to time, paced, read again.

Ana could hear the music as she scrubbed the bathroom floor, her bony knees aching as she knelt on the cold tiles. She dipped the wooden scrub brush, bristles bent from overuse, into a red plastic bucket a quarter full of water, then pushed the brush across the black-and-white floor. She had always wondered whether the black squares were placed first, or the white, whether the white ones jumped out at you, or the black. Her stomach heaved, and she considered the fried bread they'd eaten for lunch.

So little water was available this week that one couple they knew had boiled water from the river that served as a sewer. Ana pressed hard, scouring every square inch of surface, even harder on the grout between the tiles. It looked as if black flecks had lodged in the grout, and she removed a toothbrush she had reserved for this purpose from her pocket and began scrubbing around the corners of the tiles. She dipped the toothbrush into the bucket, scrubbed again.

When she'd finished the bathroom floor, she poured the water from the bucket into the soil of the potted plants in the living room. Emir and Muhamed were watching, but she was not in the mood for conversation and took the pail into the kitchen and partially closed the door. Framed, black-and-white photographs of Muhamed at various ages clustered on the wall. She poured more water from a canister into the bucket, just enough to slosh around the sides and clean it out, then emptied the water into a tin can for use later. Some people were digging wells in their gardens in search of water. She filled the pot up again, just a quarter full, and tiptoed with it to the bathroom. A black-and-white cartoon Emir had drawn hung on the wall. Ana plopped the pail on the floor and knelt down again on the tiles, pulling an old, gray rag out of the cabinet. She dampened the rag in the bucket, wrung it out with her cracked, red hands, and began to wipe the white porcelain underbelly of the sink. She covered every speck of surface, soaking up more water with the rag and washing stubborn brown spots, then moved down the pedestal, and cleaned it from top to bottom, being careful not to let any water drip on the floor. She crawled over to the toilet and sat down cross-legged beside it, her skirt flopped carelessly in her lap, and began scouring from the floor up, cleaning the hardware meticulously.

She saw feet and looked up at Muhamed's face.

∞

Anne remembered the black-and-white tile floor in the bathroom of the train station. When she'd been attending a women's college in Virginia (after attending a girls' prep school in Virginia), she'd traveled to New York for the weekend and was washing her hands in the rest room of the train station when a short, blond, acne-faced person ran through the door and fondled her briefly before rushing out again.

Anne was confused—it looks like a man, but can't be since this is the ladies room, so it must be a lesbian.

Anne could see the person waiting for her through the open door as she prolonged the drying of her hands with the rough, brown paper towels. She looked around to the only other person in the ladies room, a black woman who hadn't seen the incident. Anne asked the woman if she would mind walking out with her, after explaining the situation.

"Of course," the woman said, and they left together. The blond man (she realized now) approached Anne, but the woman lashed out, screaming and flailing her arms wildly at him until he went away.

Anne was weak with gratitude. "I'm just not used to the city."

"I never get used to it."

❧

Ana jumped up from her seat at the outdoor café and moved one chair to the right; Muhamed quickly did the same. Four chairs were placed around the green table, a block from their apartment.

Muhamed licked his chocolate ice-cream cone energetically; the café had scored a coup on the black market. Ana rejoiced to see Muhamed engaging in such childlike behavior; it was worth the risk to bring him this moment, to make him forget her need to scrub bathroom floors with toothbrushes.

She slid her coffee cup over in front of her, and it made a grating sound as it moved across the wobbly metal table;

the coffee came close to sloshing over. Across the street, a pack of rib-revealing dogs rummaged through trash; she turned away. Sandbags leaned against the café.

The man and woman at the next table hopped over to seats at an adjoining table. They didn't speak. Was it a mother and her son, or just an old-looking wife? Why did so many women age sooner than their husbands? Ana tried to imagine them making love and saw stomachs bumping into each other. The man looked like Petar. One of the things about aging was that everyone reminded her of someone, as if there were a limited number of physical types and now they were repeating. She was distressed at this restriction on possibility.

She remembered the day so long ago, the baby not placed in her arms.

"Chocolate chip," she said.

"Insufficient chocolate." Muhamed sucked off the top of his softened ice cream, his legs swinging back and forth in cheery rhythm.

"The chocolate is consolidated, intensified," she said.

She jumped up from her chair and moved one seat to the left, and Muhamed followed suit, eyes focused on the cone. The latticed metal chairs were uncomfortable anyway, it wasn't much trouble to move. She wondered if they had imprints on their bottoms.

Muhamed's long eyelashes fluttered with concentration, ice cream on the tip of his nose. When had she been this happy?

"Fudge ripple," she said.

"Insufficient chocolate," he said.

The man and woman at the other table returned to their original table. The woman moved slowly, hunched over. Osteoporosis, perhaps. The man's nose was aquiline.

"If you poured chocolate sauce over the fudge ripple, that would be promising," Muhamed said.

"Would you need a cherry?"

"A distraction."

"Nuts?"

"Incompatible."

They stood up simultaneously and exchanged places, never staying in one chair long enough to allow for careful aim.

❧

Anne used to love the outdoor cafés of Europe, particularly drinking café au lait in Paris, an unopened Herald Tribune *on her lap, but she didn't drink coffee anymore, or alcohol. Although she no longer tied cheap orange scarves around her neck, she smoked a pipe in public.*

She thought she heard something and looked through the peephole of the front door, making sure the alarm was on. The salesman had convinced her, easily, to pay extra for a special alarm in case the phone wires were cut.

At hotels, she leaned a chair against the door, then added glasses and ashtrays to help with sound.

❧

Sound. Ana woke suddenly with the feeling that something was wrong; the shooting had stopped.

It seemed to Ana that she never slept, although she knew that couldn't be true. Nisveta's snores sounded like a cat throwing up. The eighty-year-old woman's chest heaved and fell, the snores waxed and waned, sputtering a little toward the end. Ana, Emir, Muhamed, Mira, Nisveta, and the Zaimovic family—father, mother, son— were sleeping in the dank, dark cellar of their apartment building. Ana wondered where Petar slept, in what country. Emir had dragged them through a rousing medley of songs before retiring.

She would tell him about the baby tomorrow. Her stomach contracted.

"I *need* to," Damir was saying in his loud, raspy whisper. Emir and the others stirred at the sound. This happened every night.

"You'll have to wait," Ana mouthed the words silently to herself as the mother said them.

"But I *need* to," Ana mouthed as Damir spoke.

Ana turned over. Why didn't they bring the boy a chamber pot, for God's sake.

As she listened to Nisveta's snores, she remembered a puppy she once had, whose puppy snores were the most beautiful music she'd ever heard. Ana's goal had been to try to assure that the dog was secure and happy—completely devoid of trauma—for the entirety of its life. What a kick in the pants to fate that would have been, to have one living creature journey through life without heartbreak. She looked over at Muhamed, twitching in his sleep.

She waited. The gunshots began. She relaxed into the mattress, lulled to sleep.

4

If Ana had heard the rain during the night, she could have put out buckets and pots to collect it. She carried the small, newspaper-wrapped parcel in her hand gingerly, so as not to crush it, as she walked down the rain-slicked streets already beginning to dry, and carefully shifted her paper bundle from one hand to the other.

Overturned and charred automobiles sprawled on the streets; an engine blown out of a vehicle sat in the middle of the road. Shot-out windows gaped from blood-splattered buildings with broken-down doors, and a couple of young men looted through a smashed store window. Ana hadn't learned to fear them.

Bright, orange-yellow flames licked a window of a darkened building; a man missing an arm and a leg rested against it. Although only July, the barren trees suggested

winter. A skeletal dog crossed the street. Green tufts
sprouted out of tin cans on balconies where people grew
vegetables. Ana had never been interested in gardens,
which struck her as a failing; she was too conceptual.

She hugged the buildings on her side of the street,
walked quickly, occasionally ran in a kind of half skip,
scurrying from one doorway to another, trying to decide
whether to speed up or linger. She was pretty sure, by following certain rules, avoiding certain parts of the city and
times of day or sections of a building or a room, by evalu-
ating the sounds of weaponry—their type and origin—that
she could avoid injury. She wore her lucky jeans. She never
left the apartment on weekends, when Serb mercenaries
were free from their other jobs and came to the surrounding hills to shoot at women and children. Every day that
Ana escaped harm strengthened her sense of security, destiny. Still, her mouth went dry as sand.

Occasional machine-gun bursts erupted from the gently sloping mountains, pink-tinged snow shining on their
tips where she used to ski, avoiding the most dangerous
trails. At a building across the street controlled by snipers,
a loaf of bread tied with string was being pulled by the
string from one apartment window to another. Ana remembered when bread had been a metaphor, and she'd
kept a favorite quotation in a carved wooden box: "If I had
but two loaves of bread, I would sell one and buy hyacinths,
to feed my soul." Less true each day.

Sandbags pressed against the first floor of the building.
A television cameraman had his blood type stencilled
above his vest pocket, B-. People were scowling, silent. She

walked by a wall with a shattered stained-glass window; the torso of Jesus had vanished.

The sound of Bach floated out of the Music Academy. An occasional white UN tank rolled past, and useless UN soldiers in flak jackets and blue helmets appeared at random. A dog ran from doorway to doorway, having learned the game.

Ana felt a pang of hunger, although it seemed she felt the hunger less and less. She felt lighter. Yesterday she'd gathered dandelions and nettles for food.

She walked by the office used by the mujahideen, where she and Emir had taken cover one day when the shelling had been particularly bad, the way they used to pop into a store during thunderstorms. A woman wearing a traditional Islamic chador, black from head to foot, performed clerical work in a corner. What could make a woman dress like that.

Ana jumped out of the way as a car full of journalists zigzagged down the street at high speed to avoid snipers, and she turned down an alley. A woman hurried in front of her, holding a package in brown paper in her right arm, and Ana wondered if they were on identical missions; they all sought secret spots. Ana shifted her newspaper-wrapped parcel back to the other hand as they passed a one-legged man on crutches, and a couple of children crouched, playing with broken glass. She rarely let Muhamed outside, and not by himself, and wondered if he went out without telling them. Emir was gone this morning. She quickened her pace.

The woman ahead of Ana unbundled her packet,

revealing a gun that she held to her temple. She pulled the trigger. The loud shot rang out and echoed through the alley as her body slumped to the ground and blood flowed silently.

Ana began to shake, and turned around and tried to walk, but her legs were barely moving, rubbery, as in a dream, her whole body trembling. She took small steps and reached a dirt plot adjacent to the alley. She leaned over to place the newspaper-wrapped feces behind a rock.

The muezzin was calling the faithful to morning prayer.

❧

Eight-year-old Anne had inhaled, while trying not to, the acrid odor of lime mixed with feces, as she squatted over a hole in the two-person latrine, a camp counselor next to her. "You use too much toilet paper," the counselor said.

Now, thirty-eight years later, Anne's toilet threatened to overflow, clogged, again, with thick, soft toilet paper, and she watched as the water level in the toilet bowl rose dangerously high. A framed picture of a sugar white sand beach with sea oats by the warm, turquoise waters of the Gulf of Mexico where she'd vacationed as a child, hung on the wall of her green marble bathroom. It's what she imagined when the relaxation experts sent her to a safe place.

❧

She returned to her novel. Anne had once thought that tragedy was God's way of getting our attention, but couldn't reconcile that with nature. Do the antelope's thoughts turn to God, with the lion's teeth at her throat?

✧

Ana had been back in the apartment just an hour when Emir came home.

She held him around the waist, half carrying him, feeling the weight of his arm across her shoulders as they stumbled into the bedroom. He grimaced as they limped toward the bed.

She couldn't believe it, they hadn't even discussed it. This was the kind of thing people talked about first. She should have paid more attention . . .

Muhamed had emerged from the bathroom—he seemed to spend an inordinate amount of time there—and watched them uneasily. There was the question of what to tell him, how to keep him from feeling at fault somehow. Perhaps there was a children's book to cover the situation. Summer in Sarajevo.

Ana and Emir reached the bed, and Emir collapsed across it, groaning with pain and relief. Ana picked up his legs and placed them lengthwise on the bed as Emir emitted little gasps, then was quiet. His eyelids quivered on his pale face, opened.

"We're supposed to use ice," he said.

They hadn't had ice in months.

"I'll bring a cold washcloth."

She whisked past Muhamed standing in the doorway, barely containing her rage.

He'd had no right.

She poured precious water over a fading gray wash-cloth. Had she ever said anything that would have led Emir to believe that this was even remotely acceptable? She squeezed excess water out of the cloth and returned to the bedroom, practically running over Muhamed, and pulled a chair up to the bed and sat down, looking back at Muhamed.

"Muhamed, would you please go draw a picture of a fir tree?"

He nodded dejectedly and turned away. The walls were papered with drawings created under similar circumstances; she supposed the need for privacy could be handled in a more forthright manner. She would think about that tomorrow.

"Could I get some water first?"

She nodded.

When Muhamed had left, she unfastened Emir's pants and slid them down his hips, as he raised himself to assist. She pulled his underpants off, and tried not to look, as she placed the wet cloth in the general area of his groin; he moved it to the correct spot.

She looked away, not soon enough. She'd seen bruising, swelling, crude stitches, black and blue. Doctors performed operations by candlelight, frequently without anesthetic, sometimes sewing up wounds with fishing lines. They must have rushed; a friend had squeezed him in between injuries.

She couldn't bear to know the details; he'd only had time for a whispered explanation when he came home. The word was so clinical: vasectomy. Like something that would happen to a splayed frog in biology class, legs nailed down to an obliging board, heart fluttering through an opened chest.

They'd never known anyone who'd had a vasectomy. He was more distressed than she'd realized, such an extreme course of action. People all around them were having babies, babies, babies, more than ever. A traditional sense of destiny prevailed—if a baby were born, there would be food enough. Emir was not a traditionalist.

"Mother, would this be a tall fir tree?" Muhamed shouted from the living room.

She would never forgive him.

"Medium to tall," she called back.

"I've got some old cologne," Emir said. "With alcohol in it. To prevent infection."

Possibly he was delirious.

He held one hand on the washcloth and took Ana's hand with the other. "Look at me."

She turned slowly toward him.

Ana took her hand from his and slapped him across the face; red streaks ran up his cheek.

He gazed at the boarded-up window.

Ana held her hands over her mouth.

Eventually the cries subsided, became intermittent, stopped. She took a deep breath and slumped in the chair, so heavy, staring at her dirty feet. She felt tied up, in a small closet. She had felt this way before.

She looked up at Emir, then crawled into bed beside him as he moved over to accommodate her. The bed sagged.

"I'd wanted a girl named Mira," she said.

"A boy named Emir."

They were silent.

She rubbed her index finger in circles around the top button of his shirt.

"Is Muhamed still going to be a mathematician?" he asked.

"A pianist."

"Classical?"

"I'm discussing jazz."

"We need to get the piano tuned."

"The piano tuner is afraid to leave his apartment."

"We'll take the piano to him."

"We'll take the windows to the glass factory."

"We'll go sunbathing on the roof."

A loud thump sounded in the next room. Ana sprang out of bed and ran into the living room.

Muhamed had collapsed in a heap on the floor.

❧

Anne threw her pen down and raced to the phone; she got the number from Directory Assistance. The telephone cord snarled irretrievably.

"Senator Kennedy's office," a young girl said. Anne remembered when Muhamed had first appeared to her. He'd stared at her with large black eyes. I'm the one, he said. I'm the one for you.

"My name is Anne Raynard, I live in Cambridge, and I called about Bosnia. I called to say it's imperative that we . . . that we . . ."

"Take action?" the young girl asked sweetly.

"Yes!"

Anne imagined two columns on a piece of paper labeled "Bosnia," a check mark being applied to the "Take Action" column.

The brilliance of it. Not having to be specific. Or suffer consequences.

❧

Ana raced to Muhamed, who lay still on the floor where he'd crumpled like a rag doll, arms and legs scattered inappropriately, one hand thrown to the red oriental rug.

"Muhamed!" She shook his shoulders lightly, to no effect. His blue- and green-checked shirt tucked tidily into the blue corduroy pants, his eyes closed. The strength drained from her body—where did she end and he begin?

Emir limped up behind her, pulling his pants on, and pushed her aside. He picked up Muhamed's arm and felt the pulse as Ana watched Muhamed's tiny chest gently rise and fall. He opened his eyes.

She shoved Emir out of the way, almost slamming him into the black wood-burning stove, and leaned over Muhamed, placing a hand on either side of his face. "You're all right?"

"Certainly."

She examined the length of his body, from head to toe, checking for exit wounds.

"What happened?" she asked.

"Of that I'm uncertain."

No traces of blood.

Muhamed looked at his parents' faces. "It's all right."

Ana lifted and hugged him. She saw the shape of his body in the thick dust on the floor, the way they used to make animal prints in snow. Muhamed tolerated Ana's hug—she knew she was being tolerated; he had reached an age where he no longer sought nor seemed to take pleasure in the snuggling that had once been their mainstay. He breathed a little easier when she was satiated and released him.

"Perhaps we should sit on the sofa," he said.

Ana remained where she was. "Were you feeling ill before you fell?"

Muhamed rose and sat on the sofa. "No."

"What were you doing right before you fell?"

"Drawing a fir tree, of course."

Ana looked at Emir, who had nothing to contribute.

"I fainted," Muhamed said. "A common occurrence. You should order me to bed, to rest, and give me liquids. By morning, you will be reassured of the insignificance of the event."

Ana felt the tension leaking from her body; they were strong again. Muhamed rose and walked determinedly into his bedroom, with Ana close behind in an unnecessary gesture of supervision.

❧

Eric lay sprawled across the couch, his dyed red hair against the white cushion. Anne had convinced her son that he had a bad cold, not flesh-eating bacteria.

She had persuaded herself that well-meaning friends discouraging her from writing about Bosnia were Satanic voices.

Was it Gardner who said, if we write only what we know, we are secretaries to life? Anne was having the kind of day where, if you open a cupboard, things tumble out.

"I wonder if I can write a novel," she mused aloud. She'd once written poems, read by her mother and two friends.

Eric considered the question. "I think you'd have trouble with the cover."

Anne wondered how much of the family stubborn streak Eric had inherited. Her great-grandfather's brother, a slave-holder in Tennessee, had voted against seceding from the Union; he believed in resolving the slavery issue through compensation. After the voice vote in his small town, he was chained to the stone floor of a damp, windowless prison cell for weeks. When he was released, he formed a band of guerillas and spent the rest of the war attacking his Confederate neighbors.

Anne made a list of the pros and cons of continuing the novel, and cons outweighed pros three to one. She began the next page.

∞

The dream. In the early years it had been frequent, then sporadic. Now, every night. Ana stared at the ceiling. She turned over on her side, tried to think of something else.

She longed for simple dreams, the kind where you dreamt you had to go to the bathroom. She needed to distract herself, mark time, be quiet, so as not to wake Muhamed; everything must be organized around getting him well.

She had a flash of digging her elbows into a padded

operating table, lifting up her head. She would have to postpone telling Emir; he'd already slipped out to go to the bread line.

∞

Was bread line one or two words, Anne wondered. Was it common enough to have become one word? She'd won the fourth-grade spelling bee with Switzerland.

∞

Rats had driven them out of the cellar, and they slept in their own rooms again, although on particularly bad nights they moved to the bathroom. Ana didn't miss the basement; Damir had taken to sobbing in the middle of the night. Ana pulled her worn, pink nightgown up around her chest and touched her clitoris without enthusiasm. She rubbed gently, sliding the skin up and down, trying to establish a rhythm, then switched to tapping, patting and pressing and swirling, anything to elicit a response.

She didn't know why she even tried, and pulled her nightgown down; she brought her fingers to her nose and smelled them. If only the electricity would come on and she could use the vibrator. Ana never mentioned it to Emir, who felt it implied some sort of failure on his part, although it had nothing to do with him. It was easier for her sometimes to do it alone because she spent too much time worrying if the other person was having a good time. Sexual fulfillment, she suspected, was primarily a function of selfishness.

She wondered what Emir did when he was alone, wondered if he liked their sex life, the one they used to have. He would say so, such a nice man. If she had to guess, she'd guess he thought it was good when she was really in the mood; he probably sensed when she was composing poems. And they'd both changed over the years; now she got irritated if a strand of hair caught in their kiss, if she rolled in the wet spot. The other day he'd bumped into her breast and said, "Excuse me."

She was still thin at least, that was important, and easy now. What did he think about when he saw other women? He was very attracted to them, she knew. Did he act on it? Nothing would surprise her, but she didn't think so, if she had to bet. But nothing would surprise her. She was sure his dreams were as interesting as hers. There were mornings she laughed out loud when she woke up and realized whom she was attracted to; it was so astonishing sometimes. She had tried to explain to Emir once that, even though she had been having sex in her dream, the sex was simply a stand-in for an intellectual interaction she desired.

And what if he'd had another woman and she found out? She used to have theoretical conversations with herself about how she would react in various situations—if it had been a one-time event, if it had been a full-blown affair, if he'd been in love, if he'd been honest enough to tell her, the relative importance of honesty versus the act itself.

She felt infinitely removed from that woman. Another country.

❧

Anne's first husband had left his diary in the living room listing deeds about which he felt guilty. "Cheating on Anne" was number three. Anne spent several hours trying to persuade herself that cheating referred to cards.

When she'd met him, she'd been deeply attracted to his excesses, his every thought and act an outrage against the conventions of her youth, conventions that had rendered her helpless in the face of life's little surprises. Tall, lean Chicano with black hair and pale blue eyes. A leftover hippie, who'd dropped out of graduate school (political theory), burned out on drugs and sex in the sixties, and salved his wounds with a wide variety of uppers and downers. He worked as a sandblaster, carving names onto the black granite wall of the Vietnam Memorial.

He exuded a profound sadness, which moved her to the marrow. He could understand the depths of her own sorrow; she would save him.

He evolved into a full-blown alcoholic, and evenings were spent in terrified anticipation of his arrival, or absence. When he was drunk, he threw sharpened knives, with Freddy Fender turned up full volume on the stereo, and held a knife to the throat of his green and yellow parrot, Moctezuma, who shrieked, "Darlene!" repeatedly.

Anne's awareness of her husband's infidelity unleashed a dormant rage that howled and shook the house for weeks until he left, saying he didn't want a divorce. She divorced him. She said she never wanted to see him again and took to her bed, unable to breathe. He found a girlfriend immediately (beforehand?) and bragged about how much they had in common. It took her months, but Anne finally gathered her splintered heart in her hands and found the courage to ask what it was he had in common with his new love. "She doesn't like art either," he said.

Years later he called to apologize. "I was a jackass," he said. "Everything was my fault."

"We all made mistakes," she murmured, as if the marriage had been a committee.

∾

Ana got out of bed and moved to the suitcase. She sat down cross-legged on the floor beside the gray satchel she kept by the door, as her knees made a two-poled tent of her nightgown.

She popped the top of the suitcase open and began to finger the contents—their university diplomas, passports, her grandmother's necklace, a thermos, a blanket, spare clothes, cans of paté, toiletries, zwieback, photographs. They would have to hide money in their clothes; thank God for the royalties from Emir's plays. She wanted to bring a book, but every time she tried to decide which, she became paralyzed, and delayed, telling herself that their building wouldn't be shelled for another twenty-four hours. She leaned toward Tolstoy, while Emir suggested Beckett. She included a copy of her latest poem, which she replaced with a new one every few days.

Ana put everything back in its place and snapped the case shut, then ran her hand reassuringly across the top and set it upright again, handle at the ready. She thought of places the suitcase had gone—Paris, London, Tuscany, Greece. She'd always packed hurriedly, casually, knowing she could obtain whatever she needed at her destination and return for anything of value.

She moved to her desk, where the candle remained unlit. The hard seat of the wooden chair chilled her through the nightgown.

"Through the fog a face . . . ," she wrote. Terrible. Even the handwriting was pathetic, shaky. She'd do better tomorrow. We never saw Akhmatova's first drafts, she comforted herself.

She looked up at the piece of paper taped to the shelf above the desk. Emir had taken to affixing excerpts from Anne Frank's diary all over the apartment, saying it inspired him.

Everyone here is dreading the great terror known as winter.

Anne Frank

✎

Ana picked up the Chance cards.

Twenty-four hours had passed, and Muhamed seemed fine. Twenty-four more, and she would be sure.

After shuffling them, she placed the orange cards facedown on their allotted space and straightened the stack, patting them on top. Emir selected the silver token shaped like a wheelbarrow. "For water lines," he said. Ana had seen a man carrying water canisters in a baby carriage yesterday.

She took the token shaped like a cannon, Muhamed picked the battleship.

"They're screening *Potemkin* at the university on Wednesday," Emir said.

Muhamed was always the banker and passed out money. "I need to pee," he said, and left the table. He drank so much water. Ana had seen a movie where people had been forced to drink their own urine to quench their thirst.

She placed the bills in neat piles—yellow $500s, green $100s, pink $50s, gold $20s, orange $10s, white $5s, and blue $1s. She tried to remember how many dinars $1,500 would be. Last week she'd seen a woman spit on a dollar.

She rose to light a precious candle; the dark arrived sooner now. If they played long enough, they could eat up all the time until bedtime, although she hated to hurry the dream.

She placed the candle on the kitchen counter, keeping it away from the plywood-covered hole in the wall created by last week's shelling. Emir had painted a trellis of peach-colored roses on the wood.

Ana returned to the table, stepping around the stacks of firewood saved for winter. A couple of green branches poked out from the pile; green wood burned more slowly, giving off more smoke than heat, depositing a thin layer of soot over the contents of the room.

Muhamed returned and threw the dice. She no longer grilled him about washing his hands every time; water was so scarce, who knew its best use? Hepatitis was on the increase.

His white, terry-cloth bathrobe was frayed but, still, the contrast with his dark hair was nice. His eleven beat out Ana's six and Emir's seven, and he placed his battleship on the alarmingly red Go and threw the dice again. Three. He landed on purple Baltic Avenue, which he promptly bought for the requisite $60, the cheapest piece of property. It could have been Balkan.

Her cannon touched down on a Chance box, and she drew an orange card that said, "Make general repairs on your property."

Emir's wheelbarrow landed on Community Chest, and he drew a yellow card. "You are assessed for street repairs." When had his arms become so spindly, like an old man's?

Muhamed moved on to pale blue Vermont Avenue, which he bought.

Ver mont, green mountain. She wondered if Vermont was like Bosnia. She set down in jail, in the visitors section, fortunately.

There was a chocolate stain by the Chance cards; they used to eat ice cream when they played.

The wheelbarrow moved to the Electric Company square, and Emir bought it hungrily.

Muhamed's battleship landed on Community Chest. "Xmas Fund matures, collect $100."

"Do they have a Ramadan Fund?" he asked.

"Monopoly is a Christian game."

The room shook with explosive sound, and they held onto the table and waited, as plaster dust, like snow, fell gently on the board. You'd think the terror would diminish. She'd felt like this once when she'd been smoking pot, a kind of generalized apprehension, not attributable to a specific, single stimulus.

Ana, too, arrived at Community Chest and examined the yellow card: "You have won second prize in a beauty contest." She slipped the card under her leg and drew another. Muhamed and Emir exchanged glances but didn't say anything. "You have inherited $100."

"Will we inherit anything from Gran and Papa?" Muhamed asked.

"Bad tempers, good hair, an inability to fit in." Emir's parents had retired in Dubrovnik, hers had died years ago. Ana's father had been a serious communist, an ideologue. Her brother was a computer analyst in Massachusetts.

She could feel the card under her leg. "Who's the prettiest person we know?"

"Princess Stephanie," Muhamed said.

"We don't know Princess Stephanie."

"Anne Frank and her family played Monopoly," Emir said. "It was on April 7, 1944."

She heard shrieks. Were they out loud?

Emir moved to Free Parking. Muhamed purchased Water Works, and Ana's cannon landed on Jail, and she was in jail for real. She had hoped for Park Place. Being rich had appealed vaguely, but not enough to marry a rich man, not enough to give up writing poetry.

"I met the people who moved into Mesa's apartment," she said. The Muslim woman had hidden a Jewish family in her apartment during World War II. The family survived and emigrated to Israel after the war. When the siege of Sarajevo began, they notified Israeli authorities, and one day an El Al plane appeared in Sarajevo and spirited Mesa and her family away to safety.

"They have very bad manners," Muhamed said of the new tenants.

"They're not from here, they've had a terrible time." Refugees had moved into Petar's apartment as well.

"Would they like to play Monopoly?"

"I got a letter out to the states," Emir said. "Responses can go through that journalist. I should hear any day."

"I need to pee," Muhamed said.

Emir collected $50 from each of them as a result of a Grand Opera Opening. "What was the name of the Menotti opera we saw last year?" Ana asked.

"Muhamed, why don't you keep a diary?" Emir said. Muhamed was hit by a Luxury Tax, but was able to buy Indiana Avenue.

She'd go crazy if she couldn't remember the name of the opera. She'd always planned to take the time to see more opera. The right half of her skull was tight.

"I want to buy houses for Baltic, Vermont, and Indiana Avenues," Muhamed said. The closed room was stifling.

"You can't," Emir said. "They're not in the same color group. They have to stay with their group." The candle flamed momentarily higher.

"Why should it make a difference what group they're in?" Ana asked. Her tenure in jail was making her testy. "Let's mix up the groups!" she sang out gaily. She grabbed a handful of the colored property deeds, scrambled them, and threw them up into the air. "Whee!"

"It's the rules!"

"But who *made* the rules? You're always following rules!"

Completely unfair. Too late. Muhamed coughed loudly. Emir stood. "*I'm* not the one who renewed her driver's license in the middle of a goddamn war!"

"I need to pee," Muhamed said.

Ana stood, too, and shoved Emir. "If you weren't such a goddamn aesthete, maybe you'd be taking shots at the enemy instead of at me!"

Worse than the last time they'd argued, when she'd merely called him, unoriginally, a Nazi. These things were generational; Muhamed's wife would call him a Serb when they fought. It would have bumbling, bestial connotations, none of the German precision. No one would take the time to refine, to distinguish between Serbs.

"I've won," Muhamed said matter of factly. "It says so right here." He read from the rule book: "The last player left in the game wins."

The sharp crack of a rifle was followed by rapid machine-gun fire, sounds as familiar as traffic. The building rattled and shook, and before Ana could fashion a rapprochement with Emir, Muhamed collapsed across Pennsylvania Avenue, sending the dice rolling helter-skelter.

∞

Anne shuddered, as if in remembered pain, as she read detailed, end-to-end accounts of imaginative atrocities. Yet the writing in some of the Bosnia books, the imposition of aesthetic order, was beautiful. A well-described tragedy cheered her up, and she questioned the appropriateness of her response, and danced around the edges of the moral issues raised, not the least of which was her exploitation of Ana's life for her own purposes.

She checked books out of the Cambridge Public Library, where tattered, homeless-looking writers fought and huddled over the single copy of Publishers Weekly. *If one wanted to peruse the fat, dog-eared* Literary Market Place, *with names and addresses of agents, you had to surrender your driver's license or firstborn son to the reference desk, where a librarian explained to a caller that she couldn't do his homework. A woman in a corner muttered softly. A high school teacher revealed his reliance on Cliff Notes.*

Anne returned home and hung a wall calendar in the hall, noting all of the critical dates in Yugoslav history on pages interspersed with glossy colored photographs of endangered wildlife.

A four-foot, stuffed black gorilla sat on the oriental rug in front of a wall of books in her study; books were arranged in categories like Bosnia, Anne Frank, Islam, self-defense. She couldn't remember where she'd placed her Alzheimer's file. Sunlight streaming through the window had bleached a strip on the back of the gorilla's head, turning the fur punk-purple, and the gorilla sat with head bowed, perplexed by her toes, under a map of Sarajevo.

Anne's computer stood in the center of the large black desk next to the bronze trash can, which had to remain elevated out of Margaret's reach. Anne had downloaded a picture of the National Library in Sarajevo, a stunningly beautiful fusion of Ottoman and Austro-Hungarian architecture, from the Internet. Keyword Bosnia had yielded 125,807 items.

❧

She studied the first four chapters of her novel, which her mother said didn't depress her because she didn't think it would happen to her. Anne included no detail in her novel about which she had not read, its existence in a Sarajevo apartment or life verified. She scoured the newspapers for names, and her characters shared a disproportionately high number of names with war criminals.

Her heart stopped when a floorboard creaked.

5

Juvenile Onset Diabetes. Ana found it in her old, blue medical book, smudged and worn, but not yet consigned to burning. The doctor had explained, but now she was having trouble remembering everything. Diet important, stress bad. Comas.

She read quickly, looking for the section that would explain what to do if one lived in a city under siege, where insulin was unavailable. The book made assumptions.

❧

Ana tightened the sheets around Muhamed. Why couldn't she be the one who was ill? "Are you still thirsty?" she asked, glancing at the empty glass on the table.

He shook his head.

"When you start feeling worse, you'll tell me?" she asked.

"Of course." He didn't look at her.

"You don't need to protect me."

He was silent.

"I can manage, you know."

With great difficulty, he pulled his arm out of his swaddling clothes and scratched his forehead, then placed his hand on hers and patted it.

"When I was a girl, I had a parakeet," she said. "Its name was Duddi."

"Why Duddi?"

"My mother suggested the name. I didn't want to hurt her feelings."

"I see."

"One day Duddi died. It was my fault."

"Parakeets die. It had nothing to do with you."

"My father flushed it down the toilet."

Ana tucked the sheets under Muhamed's sides, like a mummy, and noticed the piece of paper taped to the headboard of his bed:

I also have a brand-new prescription for gunfire jitters: When the shooting gets loud, proceed to the nearest wooden staircase. Run up and down a few times, making sure to stumble at least once. What with the scratches and the noise of running and falling, you won't even be able to hear the shooting, much less worry about it.

Anne Frank

Muhamed watched her reading Emir's scribbles. "Why does he write about something so sad?" he asked.

"To say it's important." She kissed him on the forehead and looked around the room. "Would you like a pet when this is over?"

"If you like."

"We could get a puppy! We could name her Duddi!"

"All right," Muhamed said flatly.

She hugged him tightly, deeply moved by the concurrence of their desires.

∾

Ana had succeeded. Sometimes she was able to wake herself from a dream she wished to escape. Frequently she simply walked out on the rejected dream and moved into another, dreaming that she'd woken up.

That was the case this time—she found herself in bed in her childhood home, under the pale blue coverlet her mother had knitted. She pushed herself to wake again, this time landing in her adult bed with a six-foot frog squatting beside her. The frog's chest had been sliced open, its gargantuan heart pulsing. She forced another awakening.

In her own bed, a pitch black room, Emir lumped in shadow beside her. She studied the outline of his sleeping form; he slept on his side, facing away from her.

One, two, three! She threw off the covers and moved quickly to the desk, placing her hands on the matches and candle effortlessly. She lit the candle, and was startled by the hulking figure on the wall, her wild, unkempt hair protruding like a troll's.

Emir raised up slightly before collapsing back on the bed.

"A dream," she said. She ran back to the bed and crawled under the covers.

"I'm sorry," Emir said, not moving. Nightmares were routine.

She waited.

Emir turned over to face her, his eyes blinking. "Do we have to waste the candle?"

She was silent.

He slowly dragged himself up to a sitting position, placing a pillow between his back and the blond headboard, leaning against it, and pulled the covers up toward his chin, as Ana grabbed them instinctively, protecting her side. Emir wore a gray T-shirt. His hair was askew, even his face awry.

Ana sat up, too, waited.

"What," he said.

"This will be difficult."

"Ana!"

She pulled on her fingernails.

"I was pregnant."

Emir straightened, and turned toward her.

"When I was sixteen."

Emir studied her, then shifted and looked across the room.

Ana sank the fingernails of her left hand into the palm of her right, then looked up at Emir. "The baby was adopted." The lengths her family had gone to to keep the secret.

Emir examined the far wall.

Ana held herself. "I've been having dreams, since the vasectomy, since Muhamed got sick."

War had brought her here. Her first child was linked to Muhamed in ways she could not articulate, as if the safety of one depended on the safety of the other. She was surrounded by loss; she would lose nothing more. She would regain.

She stared at Emir's profile, the delicate tip of the nose belying the strength of the jaw, and put a hand on his shoulder, letting it slide down his arm.

Emir scratched his beard and got out of bed. "I'm going to be the first person in the water line."

Ana watched him dress and leave. She rolled over to his side of the bed, soaked up what warmth remained.

She would find the child. Sooner or later.

❧

Ana faced Zijo, whose black-market credentials were impeccable.

"Some months we have insulin, some we don't," he said.

How had he managed to remain so portly. His full black beard spilled over his jowls, and in spite of the beard, he shaved off his mustache, an aesthetic Ana never understood.

"Not this month."

Someone with dark hair was sitting in Zijo's back room, the door cracked, listening probably. Everything seemed just out of reach.

"I have gold earrings," she said, fingering her mother's earrings in her pocket.

"It isn't a matter of price." He laughed delightedly at the idea that he would turn down a sale. A newspaper on the counter was open to the obituaries.

❧

Ana stood with Emir in a room at the Holiday Inn. A single, unmade bed pressed against a table with a computer and telephone; books, papers, and clothes were strewn all over the floor, an ashtray overflowed with cigarette butts.

A copy of *Black Lamb and Grey Falcon* lay on the bed. Sunlight streamed through the open window, which faced away from snipers.

The journalist, Barry Fairfax, got off the phone. "If they brought insulin for you, that would be seen as taking sides. They need to remain neutral."

A wine stain bloomed between the second and third button of his shirt.

A red-haired man with a camera—Ana recognized him as the American television cameraman who'd shot video footage of her at Sniper Alley—stuck his head in the room and took their picture.

Barry gathered his things and started out of the room, then turned. "Would you like some gum?"

Ana wanted the gum.

❧

Anne cringed when her knee rubbed up against the petrified gum stuck under the wooden desk in the university class-room where the writing workshop met, and thought how the desk should be smaller, like a child's desk, since she'd been out of school for over twenty years. Eight participants rang-ing in age from eighteen to sixty-two formed a raggedy circle, and an unoccupied teacher's desk stood at the far end of the room under a chalky blackboard. The hands of a large black clock moved slowly. It was night. But not yet midnight.

The stragglers arrived, and Anne cleared her throat, al-though she wasn't allowed to speak during discussion of her novel. The horrific flaws in her manuscript had become ap-parent to her the minute she'd put it in the mailbox to send to the workshop. This happened whenever she placed a man-uscript in a mailbox, and her husband had suggested reme-dying the problem by putting a fake mailbox in their backyard.

The first day of the workshop, the leader had announced that critiques must begin with something positive. By the sec-ond meeting, everyone had forgotten.

"The spacing is wrong on page eleven," the tightly curled English major said.

Too many overhead lights hung from the ceiling in the stuffy classroom, and Anne blinked in the glare. She's getting back at me for questioning her ending. Anne felt an insect bite on her leg, but didn't move to scratch it.

"The subtlety is nice, but I wonder about accessibility."

With bowed head, Anne made a note to be more obvious. Make concessions to the uninformed reader. How dumb to go? She would make her husband the measure—smart, but not literary. Throw a few bones to the literary crowd, but not so many that the merely smart would get confused.

"No one cares about Bosnia."

It's not about Bosnia.

"Why are you so interested in Bosnia?"

Why aren't you interested in Bosnia?

"The trouble is," said an earnest, high-waisted young man, "it's just not a very appealing place to be. And why doesn't Ana exhibit some pluck and get out of the situation?"

The prop fell out of the opened window, which slammed shut.

6

Ana found Muhamed in the windowless kitchen. She observed him intently, a hundred times a day, seeking signs of invisible illness.

She prepared herself a glass of sugar water, which was supposed to help with trembling. On the way home from the Holiday Inn, an elderly woman walking ahead of them had been hit by a mortar, her legs twisted in impossible angles; it had smelled like a butcher shop. The woman's screams merged with others heard over the past few months, an acoustical tapestry that accompanied Ana everywhere.

∾

Much too grim, Anne thought. Although there was the issue of authenticity.

❧

"Guess what Damir told me?" Muhamed said. "You will find this of significant interest." Sometimes when Muhamed spoke, Ana was glad they weren't being overheard. Damir was not the friend Ana would have picked for her son in ordinary times. His parents laughed when he used bad words.

Muhamed sat down at the table. "I'm feeling a little thirsty."

She gave him a glass of water, which he guzzled. She hoped someone was bringing water for her other child; soon she would know.

Muhamed sat erectly and folded his hands on the table in front of him.

"Remember that forest in the valley where we had the picnic the day Father pretended to be a bear?"

She nodded.

"And he pretended to be a bear dancing a waltz?"

She nodded again.

"And he pretended to be a bear dancing a waltz looking for . . ."

"Muhamed!" she snapped. She forced a smile. "I'd like to hear your story."

He nodded. An objective observer might think his ears stuck out too much.

"They've been shooting in that valley where we were,"

he said. He cleared his throat in preparation for the telling of his story, and looked off into the distance, envisioning the scene.

"One day last summer—it was raining—a girl my age arrived in the valley carrying a small bundle wrapped in brown paper.

"She came up to Mirsid, one of our soldiers, and asked for her father. Her mother had sent her with her father's supper and a sweater. When she told Mirsid her father's name was Dragan, Mirsid said he was on the other side.

"The girl began to tremble, her whole body was shaking, and tears fell on her face.

"Mirsid called over to the other side and told them the girl was coming.

"Nobody shot while the girl ran over and found her father."

Ana took a sip of sugar water.

"Some time later, the girl's father shouted that she was returning. Again, the guns stood silent while the girl ran back.

"She brought coffee to Mirsid, and told him that her father had said they wouldn't shoot anymore that night, but that the next day new troops were coming—they weren't from Sarajevo—and there would be the worst shooting they'd ever seen.

"It happened just that way."

When Muhamed had finished, he sat quietly, looking up at Ana.

She studied him. "That little girl must have been very frightened."

❧

Insanity. On a treacherous, secret route, Ana had brought Muhamed to the zoo. She would will normality. The look on his face in the kitchen had sent knives through her heart.

Muhamed had caught her passion—her pleasure was his pleasure—and walked quickly, happily through the entrance to the zoo, holding her hand, onto the deserted grounds, where even zookeepers faced the threat of snipers.

Ana chased danger from her mind. It was quiet today, the gunfire sounded far away, and mist hung on the mountains, hindering visibility.

A child should be able to visit the zoo, both of her children. She was more certain of that fact than of any she'd ever known, more determined to make it true. Soon her children would be able to come together. She would listen to the warning sounds, seek cover if the shots from the surrounding hills came close.

A lone birch tree stood tall at the crest of a hill, and Ana walked over to it, fondling it, sliding her fingers along the white bark as if it were silk.

Muhamed hopped from one foot to another, grinning. "It's even verdant!" he said, pointing to the foliage. His vocabulary embarrassed her, but no one heard.

"Let's stay here for a few minutes," she said, sitting cross-legged and leaning up against the tree. Muhamed joined her.

She looked up at the pure blue sky backing the pale green leaves, a puff of white cloud. Zoos smell like Roquefort cheese.

A white swan wandered through the park, sparkling in the brilliant sunlight. What a glorious day! Ana and Muhamed watched its small steps of uncertain destination. A rose peeked out from a scraggly bush.

When she was a girl, Ana's parents had allowed her to pick something special to do on her birthday, and she had always picked the zoo; even as an adult she loved it.

Muhamed had never picked the zoo, she realized, once selecting the symphony, another time the science fair.

"Do you like the zoo?"

"Of course."

"What do you like about it?"

"The design of the cages."

She picked up a gnarled twig and beat it against the ground. Emir had always liked the interaction between the animals and the keepers. He was at the post office, hoping for word from America, and Ana tensed as she thought about how angry he would be if he knew they were here, although she had picked a good day for this forlorn terrain; it was as if the snipers had abandoned their vigil, with no one here to harass.

She looked down at her belt, hanging loosely at the waist, and moved it over another notch.

A pony appeared, walking down the path like a human. Perfectly wonderful.

Muhamed seemed concerned. "Shall we go see the cages now?" she asked. He nodded, stood, and took her hand when she got up.

As they made their way to the wild animals, a shrieking monkey ran across their path. Weeds grew over the walkway.

The wolf pens were first. They must be in their dens—she didn't see them. As a child, she'd had nightmares about wolves; they'd hidden under her bed, in the closet. She paused at the cage long enough for Muhamed to study it, and as her eyes moved across the space, she saw a furry heap on the ground in the back.

She pulled on Muhamed's hand and jerked him away. "Lions!"

"I'm thirsty," he said.

The lion cage was still; the heat, she supposed; they probably moved as little as possible. When she saw a lion lying prone in the corner of the cage, flies buzzing around its ratty, matted mane, a slow horror crept along her skin and penetrated bone.

Muhamed looked up at her anxiously.

She dragged him to the next cage. *Surely not!*

The tigers lay unmoving, all ribs and flapping skin.

Panthers, giraffes. Starvation was so silent.

Ana bent over, thrusting her head between her legs so the blood would return.

After a few seconds she stood, grabbed Muhamed, and ran with him toward the exit, past the pony, past the swan. Past the peacock standing guard beside its dead mate.

∞

Ana played with the well-worn, stuffed brown bear in Mira's bedroom, cupping its ears, running her index finger across the brown plastic nose with black stitching. "What's his name?"

"Tito." Mira was pulling out her dresser drawers one by one, rummaging through them, then slamming them shut. She wore the gold lily earrings Ana had always coveted. "Why did you happen to think of it now?"

"Winter."

"Not for three months."

Mira turned around with the turquoise sweater Ana had lent her last winter.

Ana put it on and returned to her seat on the rocking chair, rocking slowly, wrapping her arms around herself.

"Do you remember when we were nine and I got that doll with the tight black pants and high heels?" Ana said.

"A white brocade jacket."

"When did we switch from wanting baby dolls we could cuddle to wanting grown-up dolls we could be?" Ana hugged the bear. How could she protect her first child from this war if she didn't know where it was?

Mira walked over to a shelf by the window and picked up a barrette; the window threw a square of sunlight on the wood floor, highlighting the thick layer of dust. Mira pulled her hair behind her head and clasped it.

Muhamed had seemed particularly tired this morning.

"Were you ever in love with Emir?" Ana asked.

"He had holes in his socks."

"If something happened to me, I'd want you to take care of Muhamed."

Mira turned away, glanced out the window.

"I went to Zijo's yesterday," Ana said. "There's nothing in his store anymore, of course."

She rocked rapidly, not mentioning the man shot in the street, his shrieks for help, her paralysis.

"I put our loaf of bread on the counter. Zijo went into the storeroom in the back and returned with a half pint of vodka, which he gave me in exchange for the bread. And my earrings. Mostly my earrings."

Ana took a Kleenex out of her pocket and blew her nose, then returned the Kleenex to the pocket, chilled, in spite of sun, sweater.

"What happened to the vodka?" Mira asked.

"I poured it into the river. Maybe it will dilute the blood." Ana started laughing. Laughing, laughing.

Mira came over, knelt, embraced her.

Ana heard the whistle of the bullet.

Mira didn't.

∞

"We're a long way from home," Anne's father said.

Anne got off the phone and looked down at her watch; it was time. She squinted at the watch, trying to squish it like a clock in a Dali painting. Tomorrow she would have time to work on her novel. She'd dropped out of the workshop, after buying all of the participants subscriptions to the New York Times. Even her husband had gently suggested that she write a memoir.

Anne pulled the black chenille sweater over her head and pushed her arms through. As a girl, she'd worn baggy cardigan sweaters and walked hunched over when she developed breasts. She turned and looked in the full-length mirror, yanking the sleeves of the sweater up to her elbows to hide the hole in the left sleeve. The sweater was long, a tunic really, which masked her short-waistedness. She'd never known she was short-waisted until her first lover told her. Last year a doctor had asked her how long her right breast had been larger than her left. This year a doctor had asked if she were still having regular periods, and responded, "Good for you!" when she said yes. She'd wanted to ask him if he was still getting it up.

"Do I have to wear a tie?" Craig shouted from the bathroom.

"I think a jacket would be enough," Anne said.

"Could I wear cords?" Her husband had to wear a suit and tie during the week and spent the weekends negotiating down.

"Slacks would be better, but you could wear loafers if you like." When he was feeling really low, she let him wear his cowboy boots.

"You look great," he said, entering the room. They both rushed to be the first to say, "You look great," since she had explained that the responding, "You, too," was highly suspect and didn't count.

But he did look great, and she was stunned again by the good fortune of getting it right this time. She removed a strand of hair from his shoulder—his or hers?—and patted him. Craig had a first wife, but Anne wasn't threatened because the woman began letters with, "Spring is in the air."

A faint crack in the wall behind Craig led to a painting of a man casting a butterfly net from a sampan. Craig had bought it in Vietnam in 1968.

Anne bumped into the door, trying for a last look in the mirror. The carpenter thought he'd misunderstood when she asked for a lock on the bedroom door.

7

Ana and Emir were walking back from the Holiday Inn, where Barry, the journalist, had let them use his phone to call Mira's mother in Zagreb. The red-haired American television cameraman they'd seen in Barry's room before, the one who'd taped her at Sniper Alley, had been sitting on the floor loading his camera.

On the way over, Ana and Emir had practiced telling a mother that her child is dead. Ana had observed that when someone called or came to report the death of a loved one, they never had to actually say the words.

Ana had pressed the receiver to her ear. "I have something to tell you," she'd said.

They stepped over downed power lines.

〰

Ana swung around and faced Anne coldly. "You won't see me cry."

Anne looked away.

∞

Ana and Emir continued walking along the Miljacka River, by the bridge where Archduke Ferdinand had been assassinated, where once beech and elm trees lined the path. A newspaper plastered to the sidewalk alternated between articles with Latin letters used by Muslims and the Cyrillic alphabet for Serbs. The pavement, ripped by craters, strewn with rubble and bullet-riddled cars among tall weeds. Gaping holes pierced the roofs of buildings; a drummer and guitarist jammed in a basement. The hills where they used to hike rose behind boarded-up storefronts.

At the market the previous week, Ana had hidden the only available jacket from Mira's view, stuffing it under some socks, so she could buy it herself.

The cloudless sky smelled of rain. A restaurant sign dangled, a shred of twisted metal.

"Let's go by the post office," Emir said, his cheeks hollow. The post office had burned weeks ago.

Windows were shattered. A Cyrano de Bergerac theater bill, up for months, dripped from the wall of a building. Guns N' Roses blared from the transistor radio of a teenage boy with a small gold stud in his ear, and Ana prayed that Muhamed would grow old enough to offend them with dress and music. He was at Nisveta's apartment, better positioned than theirs.

If she had been kneeling, and Mira had been sitting.

A bloody trail led from a shell crater, and Ana wondered where the victim had gone, if he'd died. Why did everyone ask where God was during times of atrocity? Where was man?

A car zoomed the wrong way down the one-way street. Black smoke spewed skyward, visible for miles; the National Library had been shelled. Charred sheets of paper and soft gray ashes rained down on Sarajevo, and Ana captured a floating page and read a few words—a poem in Arabic meter—before it melted.

Giant, angry flames, out of control, hissing, crackling, swallowed the building on a street bathed in orange light. Graceful arches supported by gouged granite columns were visible through the flames, wavy, filmy.

Ana's eyes watered, she squinted against the smoke, her throat tickling. A human chain formed around the building, and people passed charred books from hand to hand. She remembered an overdue book.

She moved closer to the fire and held her hands up to warm them. She turned to Emir; his features blurred.

"Her hair wasn't the least bit thin," she said.

"Maybe just a little."

She buried her face in his chest.

❧

They'd barely spoken since Mira's death.

She picked up the foot of the bed as he had instructed, and carried it, following him into the living room, wincing as the sheet dragged on the dirty floor; she hadn't made beds in some time.

"Over here," Emir said, leading to the wall.

She put her end of the bed down and Emir moved the bed close against the wall, centered in the space, then stood back and studied it. Ana picked the errant sheet up from the floor and straightened the bedcovers.

"Now the other one," he said.

"Muhamed's, too?"

"It's got to be authentic."

He marched into Muhamed's bedroom, and Ana followed slowly, thankful that Muhamed was playing with Damir. Muhamed seemed weaker.

They could fit another bed into Muhamed's room; it could be the children's room.

Emir picked up the head of the bed—they had their routine down—and she lifted the foot. A piece of bedspread snagged on the wood in the doorway, but tore free as they moved through.

Emir positioned the bed in the middle of the wall adjacent to the wall with the other bed. "Good." He rubbed his palms together and looked around the room. "The stove's already here. Excellent."

He went over to the sofa and referred to a book he'd propped open. "Ah. Table. We'll bring the one from the kitchen."

He started toward the kitchen. Ana didn't question, she questioned less and less. Nothing was interesting.

She followed him into the kitchen and gripped one end of the kitchen table as he grabbed the other, and they lifted, as she moved backward through the door into the living room, trying not to look at Emir, embarrassed by their activity. The table was lighter than the bed, easier on her back.

"Here!" he shouted and plopped the table down in the center of the room. Ana dropped her side, a little too abruptly.

"Now we've got to take the sofa out," he said.

No.

"I need to be able to imagine it exactly."

Ana sat down on a chair, exhausted, muddled. Always muddled. Not knowing what day it was, what season.

"Come on!" he said.

She got up and went around to the end of the sofa. He picked up his end and she tried to pick up hers, but it was too heavy.

"I'll lift, you push," he said.

She leaned into the sofa. "Where are we taking it?"

"Our room."

There was a time when she couldn't have tolerated the feet of the sofa dragging across and marring the wood floor. The book on the sofa jiggled and slid toward her end; at one point they had to stop and move a rug out of the way.

The sofa wedged in the doorway. Emir grunted and pulled, Ana pushed. They were clear.

Emir didn't concern himself with the placement of the sofa in the bedroom, but dropped his end and ran back into the other room, while Ana sat down heavily on the sofa. She looked at the book and opened it to the page marked, studying the hand-drawn diagram of a room and its furnishings.

"Come on!" Emir shouted.

She returned to the living room.

"This is great!" Emir said. "I can see it all."

He put his hands on her arms and moved her over by one of the beds. "You be Anne and I'll be Otto Frank. When Muhamed returns, he can be Peter."

He picked up a pen and made a couple of notes on his manuscript.

∞

Anne made a last-minute note on her Ana manuscript and patted it. She went downstairs.

"We love you very much but you'll have to stay. We won't be long."

Craig ridiculed Anne for her loud, carefully enunciated explanations to the dog. Margaret was being stalked by the neighborhood cat; Anne was afraid of it, too. The dog was so small that Anne had almost killed her when she dropped a dictionary on her. Margaret was the only dog in Cambridge without a literary name, which pleased Anne, and she barked energetically if anyone neared the house.

Anne entered the newly renovated, sparkling black-and-white granite kitchen to dispose of the crumbs of her spinach croissant. She didn't know how to use the oven. She had a Croatian cleaning woman who came twice a month; she didn't speak English, so there was no need to chat. Anne moved her purse from room to room, while pretending not to, as the woman made her way through the house. The cleaning woman plopped her purse on the coffee table in the living room and never moved it.

A framed picture of Anne's son wearing dreadlocks, which he'd given her for Mother's Day, hung on the kitchen wall. When she'd visited him in jail for a marijuana-related offense, she'd tried, unsuccessfully, to resist the cliché of a hand pressed against glass. She couldn't get the shouts of the inmates out of her mind, the terror of their proximity. Tonight Eric was playing guitar at one of those clubs where you jump off the stage and are carried horizontally by masses of anonymous arms.

She flicked off the light switch as they left, as well as the mystery switch—they weren't quite certain what it controlled, but it seemed safer to leave it in the off position. Their television had developed a malfunction earlier in the day and wouldn't turn off.

"Did you lock the back door?" she asked Craig. She knew he left it open without telling her when he went running, as he couldn't let a heavy house key eat into his speed. Every door wore two locks, requiring different keys.

∞

Ana and Emir had deconstructed the Anne Frank apartment and returned the furniture to its original position. Ana moved the rocking chair into Muhamed's room and guarded him. His bed was centered on the far wall, to the left of a rough wooden dresser and bookshelf (three shelves, full). Behind her, across the pale blue, black-bordered oriental rug with pink and yellow flowers, a simple desk and chair pressed against the wall. On the planks of wood boarding up Muhamed's window, Emir had painted a snowcapped mountain above gently rolling green hills, a river cutting through. A white horse skipped over clouds.

Ana had covered the walls of the room with brightly colored posters by artists—Chagall, Rouault—whom she'd hoped would quietly penetrate and influence Muhamed. His walls, like the rest of the apartment, were stark white, the blue tone white, not the creamy, yellow, off-white; Ana had felt white-white provided the best background for the art, which must remain paramount. On the left side of the bed, a rose rug brightened the dark wooden floor. Rose was Ana's favorite color.

She supposed someday Muhamed might want to decorate the room himself. Although he had already made his impact; everything in the room was in its place, and he kept his toy box in the closet. Would he have been different if he'd been raised with a sibling?

"Would you like to change anything about your room?" she asked.

Muhamed looked around. "This is fine." He thought. "Perhaps some day we could hang equations on the wall."

He turned back to her. "You shouldn't worry about me so much."

Although they were having the first snowfall of winter—the beauty of it offended— Muhamed was wearing a white, sleeveless undershirt over his concave, little boy's chest. He said he wasn't chilly, that he didn't need to move near the stove, as if he didn't feel the cold. She was staggered by the child's vulnerability, desperate for a spare.

Above Muhamed, cracks radiated out from the wood-covered, shell-induced hole in the wall, like a giant spider web. He sat cross-legged on the bed in his underpants, cutting up maps from the atlas, destroying and rearranging national boundaries.

∞

Ana heard Emir come in and rose to meet him. He carried two canisters of water into the living room, kicking the door closed behind him, and tracked mud and snow through the room, across the parquet floor and the deep red of the busy oriental rug.

He didn't look at Ana as he proceeded to the kitchen; the neck of his gray T-shirt poked out above his green wool sweater and brown jacket. He wore black wool gloves, but his scarf had been stolen, pulled off of him by a young boy the last time he'd returned carrying a load of wood. Emir had told Ana that the boy needed it more than he did, the kind of thinking that enraged her. That had made her fall in love with him.

He placed the canisters on the white kitchen table and removed his black beret, just like the one her father used to wear. The electric stove stood uselessly on the left wall of the kitchen, and a single, upside-down ceramic bowl sat on the blue plastic drainboard.

"Were you the first person in the water line?"

"I let an elderly couple go ahead, they needed the water more."

He smelled of wet wool. She heard Muhamed playing the piano, badly out of tune.

"Is it cold?"

"The same as here." He took off his gloves and threw them on the table and hung his jacket on a chair; melting snow from the jacket dripped onto the black-and-white checked linoleum floor. He sat down on a wooden chair and began removing his wet boots, his old hiking boots, the ones he'd used to climb Mount Trebevic, and his numb fingers struggled with the profusion of laces.

Ana sat opposite him. Muhamed had stopped playing the piano. "Did you see anyone we know?" she asked.

"Vincetic."

"How's he making out?"

"His neighbor's suing him because his dog barks too loud."

Emir looked up at her, considered his words. "Your child's not a baby anymore."

He removed a recalcitrant boot, wiggled his thawing toes. "Do you know the sex?"

"I didn't see." She wondered how that sounded. It didn't matter, who could understand.

Emir stood and left the room, almost tripping over Muhamed at the door, hovering. What would Muhamed think when he found out?

Ana pulled Emir's boots toward her by the laces and slipped her feet in.

He didn't know what she had to do.

Bloodied, badly wounded patients were carried on stretchers or pushed on wheelchairs. Some drifted about in a kind of fog, arms in casts, or pulled themselves along with crutches. Moans wafted up from the mêlée.

The hospital corridor was brimming with activity as white-jacketed, bleary-eyed medical personnel made their way through the throngs; relatives and neighbors brought food for the patients. Ana took a moment to absorb the scene, trying to make sense of the stimuli, to focus. It was too early for candles to illuminate the cracked, patched walls. Nisveta had been in the hospital last week, killed by a sniper as she lay sleeping in a hospital bed by the window. Ana hoped Muhamed would never have to come here.

She approached a woman sitting behind a desk.

∽

A fire, after a shell, had destroyed records. It wasn't the birth certificate so much; Ana had hoped that there might be some clue about the adoption. She slumped onto a bench in the waiting room, leaned back against the wall, closed her eyes.

The pain had ceased suddenly, and she'd been flushed with warmth. Ana had raised her head, propping herself up on elbows digging into the operating table, hungry for the first glimpse. She peered through the valley of her thighs to the indecipherable mass of flesh and blood and mucus and the white arms of doctors and nurses moving swiftly back and forth doing whatever it is they do, the sweet sound of cries, such golden chords. Blinking the film of tears from her eyes, she strained again to see, but the tangle of white arms had enveloped the infant and carried it quickly through the door. She sank back onto the padded table, tears flowing freely now, the howls louder, someone's howls. Her torn cervix ached, and still she felt the baby's girth packed snugly within her womb, a severed limb forever hers.

Ana hadn't thought of this in years, she was good at not thinking of it. But now there was hunger and thirst and sickness and blood, dust and fire and death, and she must find her way to the child, as a leaf turns its face to the sun.

Anne's son had read parts of her novel about Ana and said it had potential.

Craig put an arm around her as they walked, slowly, to accommodate Anne's fashionable shoes—large, sculptured blocks—which formed a seamless black statement with her velvet pants. One of the joys of walking in Cambridge at night was looking into the well-lit, book-lined interiors of the yellow, pink, and white Victorian houses jammed together on narrow streets—toy town, a friend called it. Cambridge was dense with writers, and if a fire alarm sounded, everyone ran out of apartments clutching manuscripts.

She turned to Craig. "What happened at the meeting?"

"We're opening an office in Southeast Asia. They asked me to run it."

She imagined the Hanoi Hilton, then erased it and replaced it with a Pepsi billboard.

"I said no."

Last night she'd dreamed she was Ana, trying to escape Sarajevo, and got as far as Germany, but then remembered she'd forgotten something, and returned. She knew Ana had studied French literature at the university in Munich, where she'd met Emir, but didn't know how to incorporate that into the text.

"Did you read about what's his name, the writer, killed himself?" Craig asked.

"Terrible."

"It was a plastic bag."

"I could never do a plastic bag. I could do the oral stuff—pills and applesauce—but not the plastic bag."

"I don't think you suffocate."

"You must suffocate—why else would you do it? Why do we keep plastic bags away from babies and pets? It sticks to your nostrils."

"I think it's just breathing the carbon monoxide, or dioxide, like when you do it by running the car in the garage, apparently you don't have the sensation of suffocating."

"That's how I want to do it, in the garage. We'll get the garage door fixed so it won't leak. We could rent it out. Boomers, all getting old at the same time. If the bag wasn't supposed to suffocate you, why wouldn't they use another type of bag, like paper?" She wondered if they had garages in Sarajevo.

A miracle—she'd been able to communicate with residents of Sarajevo online; the Internet had broken the siege. She had verified details of diet, property damage, and casualties. Ana and Emir didn't have a computer. "I don't know where I am or where I'm going," Anne's father had said.

She looked in the shadows. A year ago, Anne had felt wonderful, on a beautiful spring morning in the Green Mountains of Vermont, taking a long walk before breakfast, basking in the warmth of the sun, the wind against her face. She saw a kind-looking white-haired man by the side of the road as she walked past briskly. Robert Frost. Perfect. "Beautiful morning, isn't it?" he said. "Beautiful!" she replied. "You look great without a bra," he said, gunning his pickup and taking off.

A bumper sticker said, "I'd rather be smashing imperialism." They were approaching one of her favorite houses and saw a teenaged boy being led away in handcuffs by the police. Anne looked through a window of the house into the

high-ceilinged dining room, at what appeared to be his parents,
embracing and crying. It was a beautiful, large house—a man-
sion, really—set far back from the street. Very French-looking,
ivy-covered balconied stucco with columns, pale blue shutters,
stone urns with sculptured plants at the entrance, a lengthy,
winding driveway through antique sycamore trees, a shiny
black wrought-iron gate. Anne had often thought how nice it
would be to live there.

She heard footsteps behind her and turned. No one.

Cambridge was crawling with students, and she frequently saw couples kissing passionately in the middle of side-
walks, or streets, as pedestrians and traffic swirled around
them. Anne tried to remember if she'd ever felt that way,
oblivious to her surroundings.

When she left evening readings, she ran down the middle
of poorly lit streets to her parked car. She never got into an
elevator with a strange man; she'd snap her fingers as if she'd
forgotten something and walk away. A friend had been
afraid to get in an elevator with a man, but he was Filipino,
and she didn't want him to think she was a racist, so she
stepped in and he robbed her.

Anne read the Crime Watch section of the newspaper
and walked erectly, with balled fists, insistent on eye contact.
She was phobic in elevators, airplanes, the middle seat at
movies, anything suggestive of captivity.

She'd seen a film about two Muslim women who'd been
imprisoned at the Serb camp at Omarska. After the film, the
women had come onstage to answer questions standing at a
microphone, tightly clutching purses they'd been afraid to
leave backstage.

8

Muhamed sat on his bed solving math problems while Ana perched on her chair and watched him, listening to Emir playing mournfully on the piano in the living room.

She came up behind Emir, who continued playing, pausing occasionally to make a mark on the music. He stopped and inspected his notes. "It will include blues, gospel, and rock."

"No jazz?"

He shook his head. "Tap dance."

"Whom do you see playing Anne?"

"A young Isabella Rossellini."

"Is it going to be like anything I've seen?"

"Will it be derivative, you mean?" He played a few notes, stopped. Started again, stopped. "I need to know."

"Petar," she said.

He nodded, didn't seem surprised. She sat down next to him on the piano bench, facing away from the piano as he stared at the music.

"I've known him since I was three," Ana said. "Our parents were friends when we lived on Mashopic Street."

She followed his gaze to the music. Was this what he wanted to know, what did he want to know?

"We were in the same class at school. When I was eight, he socked me in the stomach and knocked my breath out; I was so proud that he'd picked me." She turned to Emir. "All the girls were crazy about him."

It was important for him to understand that, something she would have to explain. Men couldn't understand what women found attractive. He was always surprised when she mentioned someone who was, whereas she never was, she could easily persuade herself that any woman was more attractive than her. Emir had a hard time believing that his colleagues were anything but inferior.

"When I was four, we hid from our parents for two hours in a closet." She'd forgotten that, she needed to get it all in, or perhaps none of it. What did he want? She would leave out the part about playing doctor in the garden, how Petar had said God wouldn't like that, how she had said God wouldn't mind.

Emir rested his hands on the piano.

"We went ice skating once, on the river, and some boy pushed me down and stood over me, not letting me up, and Petar made him leave." This was ridiculous, why did she think it was relevant, what was relevant? She felt as if she were building a case. No, that wasn't it, she truly wanted to be understood. The futility of that deepest of human desires.

Ana glanced at the mirror in the foyer, cracked down the middle. It yielded such interesting images and was her favorite kind of art—realism, only twisted.

"When we were eight, he had a birthday party and invited only boys, except me." It poured out, as if some elusive catharsis might greet her at the end. She turned to Emir. "He wasn't fat then, you know." Emir gave no sign of having heard.

"When we became teenagers . . ."

Ana looked to Emir for help. She had a sudden yearning for the yellow wooden dog on red plastic wheels she'd had as a child; you pulled it along behind you with a string and were never alone.

She couldn't do it by herself. If he wasn't going to participate. What did he think? It occurred to her that she might have surrendered her virginity before Emir did. Sometimes she'd thought she liked sex more than Petar; it was harder for her to stop. Emir didn't seem jealous, although she couldn't be sure. He might have been, before. Jealousy had been sucked of its power.

"I didn't see him again until he moved into our building." She'd felt nothing when she saw him, after years of dread, only relief, and confusion as to what she'd seen in him in the first place, almost as if it had never happened. Although once or twice she'd found herself rubbing the small of Emir's back. That was Petar's spot.

Emir was skimming the piano keys with his fingers, dusting.

"I didn't think about the past," she said.

Emir pressed down heavily on the keys, and the deep chord echoed loudly through the room. "Thinking about the past is in vogue." He played a few bars. "Has anyone heard from Petar since he left?"

Ana shook her head and glanced at the brass-topped Ottoman coffee table, which had once supported a vase of roses—white, with just a hint of peach—that had perfumed the entire apartment. Emir had given them to her on the occasion of her twenty-ninth rejection slip. Her first, and only, collection of poems had been accepted for publication two weeks later.

"Were you surprised it was Petar?" she asked.

"Surprise is extinct."

The building groaned and shook; a rose-colored wine-glass crashed to the floor and shattered. Emir played the Yugoslavian national anthem.

Ana rose and moved to the window, removing the plywood on which Emir had painted silver birch trees, and leaned out, breathing deeply of the night. Red and green tracers lit up the sky.

She turned around.

❧

She was alone. Ana leaned back against the cracked, white porcelain wall of the tub, angling herself away from the irrelevant faucet, and closed her eyes, soaking up the luxury of four inches of water, cold, but never mind. She'd been collecting rain water for some time, had poured it from red and yellow plastic buckets into the tub as if it were emeralds and sapphires. Before, she took only showers, finding the bath concept, wallowing in one's own filth, disgusting.

She lay down in the tub and turned her head from side to side, nodded up and down, wetting all of her scalp and hair. Sitting up, she squeezed the last drops of green liquid from a plastic shampoo bottle and threw the empty bottle across the room before applying the shampoo, pushing it through the mangled strands.

The scrap of soap was cracked hard and dry—deep, dark crevices spread across the white bar, rutted roads on a neglected map. She dipped the soap in water, then brought it to her neck, visiting every part of her body, the hollow stomach and knobby knees, replenishing the moisture as needed. The enervated bar of soap yielded film, not lather.

An image of Muhamed's emaciated body floated before her. She shoved it away.

The hair on her legs and under her arms had grown long and dark. The vanity that had dogged her was now without foundation. It was a law of the universe, she supposed, that we lose that which we treasure most. God had probably designed the entire war to teach her various lessons, the suffering of others incidental to the tests prepared for her.

She leaned back again and closed her eyes, soothed by the water's slow caress, her thoughts drifting to babies, babies floating in amniotic sacs, babies emerging from the cervix, sliding gently into warm water; she'd read about women who gave birth that way. She imagined being born—her head pushing through, the shoulders free, the sounds of gunfire.

To find the child, she would have to find Petar. He had made the arrangements.

❧

Her brown hair was greasy at the roots and dry at the ends. Sandra was knitting with ugly gray wool, wool that seemed to be recycled, and knitted quickly, obsessively, never moving her eyes from her work as she sat on the gold couch, grayed with dirt, in her book-lined living room. The blond coffee table was strewn with magazines and books, none of the periodicals dated after April 1992.

"Muhamed likes macaroni better than rice," Ana said.

Sandra completed a row. Why didn't she just smoke.

"Sometimes I add nutmeg," Sandra said, eyes fixed on her knitting.

"Mmm." Ana feigned interest, not knowing how much longer she could keep this up. Much of the female conversation in Sarajevo centered on pasta recipes, everyone on the lookout for new ways of preparing limited foodstuffs. Ana hadn't liked to cook before the war, but contemplated a postwar career as a gourmet chef. She fantasized about fruit, vegetables, chocolate.

She listened to the steel needles clicking, watched the swift back and forth movement, two tiny, invisible warriors fencing madly. "Do you still see patients?"

"A few." Click, click.

"I guess people must be crazier than ever," Ana said shrilly. She had never seen Sandra professionally, but imagined Sandra was the kind who sat back coolly, without reaction, while you spilled your gut. Emotional vultures. Ana wanted to throttle people like that and felt her throttle reflex rising.

When they'd been little, Ana, Sandra, and Petar had written and performed plays for their parents. They'd been close, although Sandra was a couple of years older. Once they'd written a play about an American movie star, how had it gone? Sandra had played the maid bringing delicacies on a silver tray to the glamorous actress, played by Ana. Ana never sought the best female roles, they'd been given her. Sandra didn't mind. The knitting needles moved at breakneck speed, point counterpoint.

Petar and his sister had rarely fought, which was why it was preposterous that Sandra didn't know where Petar was.

Sandra's six-year-old daughter chased her younger brother through the living room, the boy howling with mock fear. The children were bedraggled, hair uncombed, plaids mixed with stripes. "Be good to your little brother," Sandra said to her daughter without emotion.

Ana had fought with her own brother constantly and was confused when people asked if they were close. She had no particular desire to talk with him, she would die for him. Would Muhamed be close to his sibling? He'd become quieter and quieter. She was running out of time.

Sandra's husband was gone. One didn't ask. She was probably afraid to leave the apartment for food. People could be dreadful. Ana's uncle had married a Serb, but he usually got the food and water.

"Be good to your little brother," Sandra called out like a recording, like a years-old mantra, although the children had moved into the bedroom. Click, click. The sofa on which Sandra sat had become unsprung.

"What are you knitting?" Ana asked.

"A flak jacket."

Ana shifted uneasily. Sandra didn't look well, although no one did. Ana hadn't really focused on the bloodshot eyes, the grayish tinge of the skin. Sandra was thin, but cheeks and jowls sagged.

Ana rose. "If you hear from Petar . . ."

"Be good to your little brother," Sandra called out. Click, click.

❦

His head sank deep in a pillow that threatened to swallow him. His cheeks had collapsed, accentuating high cheekbones, and his piercing brown eyes were shinier than ever, glistening buttons on a beard-stubbled face. A purplish rose-colored splotch in the shape of an anvil marked his forehead.

Ana avoided Tomislav's eyes and studied the bony fingers on the yellowed sheet. "When was the last time you saw him?"

When they'd been in high school, Tomislav and Petar had been athletes. Ana had watched them playing basketball, frightened by the unbridled, sweaty physicality. She'd been a little jealous, threatened. Her first boyfriend had been thin, anemic, safer.

"May. He brought brandy."

"Did he say he was leaving?"

"No. But when the weeks passed."

"Did he go to Vienna?" He had relatives there.

"Prague, I would think."

Of course. There was a woman. Until a few months ago, Petar had brought all of his girlfriends by for her and Emir to meet.

Ana glanced at the old poster of the Yugoslav basketball team on the wall above Tomislav's head, lingering on the tall, black-haired boy on the far right. "How's Vladimir?"

Tomislav's lip twitched. She wondered what Tomislav prayed for, an end to the war, or a cure for HIV.

❧

Ana placed the loaf of bread on the coffee table. Sandra sat on the couch with her knitting in her lap, the gray, wool blob now grown long enough to curl at her feet on the floor. Her daughter had let Ana in. Sandra's eyes darted between the bread and Ana.

Ana moved toward the door. The man ahead of her in line had received the last loaf of bread, this loaf. But when everyone in line started screaming at him—he was part Serb—he had tossed the loaf to Ana and run away.

She felt Sandra's eyes on her back.

"You want to know about the baby."

She turned.

"It was adopted by a family in a village to the east. I'll give you the name of the village."

Ana clenched the piece of paper Sandra handed her. A place, a physical place. Her child existed in geography.

"The family's name?"

Sandra had returned to her knitting.

Ana touched the top of the daughter's head, stroked the blond hair.

❧

"Bill, the American television cameraman, will take me." Ana whispered so as not to wake Muhamed. Barry had arranged it with the red-haired cameraman.

Emir sat on the piano bench. "Madness."

Yes. On the other hand, she felt compelled as she had never felt compelled before, and surely such compulsion must have logic on its side, some divine protection? She could do nothing for Muhamed, nothing but this. This was the only action she could take, and she needed action. If she found the child, safe, surely Muhamed would survive, their fates inextricably joined.

"We'll leave early in the morning," she said. "Back tomorrow night."

"I forbid you," Emir said.

Ana glanced at the piece of paper taped to the piano:

I see the eight of us in the Annex as if we were a patch of blue sky surrounded by menacing black clouds . . .

the clouds are moving in on us, and the ring between us and the approaching danger is being pulled tighter and tighter . . . in our desperate search for a way out we keep bumping into each other . . . I can only cry out and implore, "Oh, ring, ring, open wide and let us out!"

Anne Frank

∽

A bumper sticker said, "Subvert the Dominant Paradigm."

Anne stepped over dog poop. When she'd scooped up Margaret's poop this morning it had the yellowish, pebbly quality it exhibited after she'd been eating paper, and Anne realized an informed detective would be able to discern when she and Craig made love by analyzying Margaret's poop; they gave Margaret toilet paper, her favorite, to snack on when they needed to distract her. Margaret had learned the meaning of Internet online audio and would jump out of Anne's lap when the cheery "Good-bye!" sounded, knowing she had a stab at a walk. Craig called Margaret "Sweetheart," Anne called her "Sweetie." They had no terms of endearment for each other.

"Scram!" Anne shouted, breaking away from Craig and moving toward a squirrel that seemed to be attacking another squirrel on a neighbor's leafy lawn. Anne clapped her hands and stomped her feet at the offending squirrel, who looked at her in confusion—she wondered if it were rabid—before obeying her imperative and disappearing behind a maple tree. Anne had fallen out of one of her shoes and

hopped on one foot to put it on again before returning to Craig, who waited patiently, accustomed to sudden outbursts of inexplicable rage. He was equally patient when she woke up in the middle of the night screaming.

∞

Anne hated parties, but forced herself to go to every other one to which she and Craig were invited because she thought being sociable was a good thing, although she couldn't remember why. She embraced Rachel awkwardly, clutching David's signed book, Feminism in Ancient Egypt, *in one hand, and a glass of water without ice in the other. Rachel smiled in a new relationship way at Parker, her boyfriend of six months, who beamed at Rachel, then at Anne. Anne remembered that Rachel had said he was impotent. He smiled broadly.*

Parker was from Vermont. A few years ago, she and Craig had been walking in their Birkenstocks in Vermont when a red-haired man with a camera drove by in a pickup shouting, "Goddamn hippies!"

∞

Anne looked through the jumble of jeans, tweeds, and bow ties at the party, and saw Craig narrow his eyes and press his lips together, which happened when someone said something stupid. She usually compensated by chattering loudly about some new topic before Craig had a chance to say anything he really meant; Anne was a middle child. The man with whom

Craig was talking had probably said something about businessmen, not knowing Craig's occupation. She'd worried when they moved to Cambridge, her choice, that she'd make him miserable, never truly at home in Cambridge because he was a businessman, never truly at home in business because he lived in Cambridge. But he took perverse pride in the renegade status it afforded him in both communities. He would withhold information about his Peace Corps years when in Cambridge, expound on them at the office. "Why do we get lost so much?" her father had said.

A glass dropped to the floor, startling her. A stranger stood too close. Such a little thing, all it took.

A waiter passed spring rolls on a silver tray. "Hvala," she thought, thank you. And he would say, "Nema na cemu," my pleasure.

At her book party, everyone would be given a name tag with the name of a disappeared, unaccounted for, Bosnian Muslim on it.

9

Ana's back hurt from bending over in a fetal position—arms crossed as in death—under the olive tarpaulin in the back of Bill's armored car. She'd shaken so much as she listened to muffled voices that she was certain of discovery. After they'd crossed the checkpoint, she'd returned to the passenger seat. They'd been lucky; the Serbs were unpredictable, sometimes letting credentialed drivers through, other times shooting at the Red Cross.

The vehicle bounced and swayed on the rocky, rutted road, aggravating her spine, or was it the terror. Mud splashed the windshield when they drove through the deepest puddles, and patches of snow and ice lent the road and surrounding hills, covered with wintry grass, a mottled look as if they, too, sought camouflage. They passed dark pine forests, limbs bent with snow, and twisted and slipped on steep, winding mountain roads, parts of which were dirt. An occasional abandoned house, the ruins of gardens. Some of the houses appeared to be ransacked, possessions strewn around yards. They saw dead farm animals and, twice, bodies. Bill stopped to take pictures with unsettling frequency. Death tourist.

Ana was nauseated. She glanced at barren trees, wondering what fruit the future would yield, and held her breath slightly as they bumped over the road, as if she could lift herself and lighten the load in the car if they hit a mine in spite of Bill's calculated, swerving path. She sat stiffly, staring straight ahead, willing away peripheral danger, the crazed sniper. It was foggy, that was a help. Pink streaks pierced the sun-rising sky; she could see her breath. They passed a couple of families hauling possessions, and, occasionally, young men in groups of twos and threes.

Bill's red hair grew over the back of his collar and fell over his left eye; he'd removed his helmet after they left the checkpoint, although he still wore his flak jacket. Freckles splattered his face. Such an American. She wondered if he missed his post with the other photographers at Sniper Alley.

"Cigarette?" he asked.

She shook her head. She was glad she'd stopped smoking before the war, given the expense, although at times she longed for the pleasure. To die of lung cancer after a number of years, that was a door she might choose. Now cigarettes were currency; she didn't accept handouts. Her desire for alcohol had dissipated for reasons she couldn't explain.

"Road's a bit rough," he said.

Please don't talk to me.

"Born in Sarajevo?" he asked.

"Are you from Texas?"

"J.R. Ewing."

She was ashamed. "Yes. In Sarajevo."

"Bennington, Vermont." He lit a cigarette. "Most people say, is that where the college is?"

"Sorry. I don't know colleges in America. Except Harvard."

"Bennington is the Harvard of Vermont."

This was a joke? It was always a joke to them. Their lawns not bloodied by world wars, their throats not slit as they slept.

"Tell me about Bennington."

He took a puff from his cigarette. "There's a college in Bennington, Vermont. People who teach at the college live in pretty, white, wooden houses with black shutters, old houses. Although they're mostly renovated." He turned to her. "Made new. Inside at least."

She nodded.

"It's so cool the way everyone in Europe speaks English." He took another puff. "And then there are the people who don't teach at the college, the ones who work. They cook in the cafeteria and pave the roads."

"What did your father do?"

"Move snow. At the college. With a snowplow. They could use him around here."

"Your mother?"

"Don't know." His weather-beaten hands tightened around the steering wheel. "She left."

Perhaps his mother sought him now. Perhaps she hadn't realized how painful the loss would be.

"Where is she?"

"Don't know."

"Have you tried to contact her?"

"I hope she's dead."

Ana felt as if she'd been thrown across a room and rammed against a wall.

She wouldn't give in to it, she pulled her gloves up over the wrist and wiggled her toes in her boots to keep warm. "Did you always want to be a cameraman?"

"A snowplower. Then my father gave me a cheap camera."

"And that was it."

"That was it."

"What was it about photography?"

"You can fix people."

She turned to look at him. "In time," he said. "No one leaves."

Always the mother's fault. Ana braced herself as they barreled through a particularly well-defined rut and wondered what kind of mother her child had. A girl, she thought. Ana imagined her daughter blond, with thick hair, like Petar's, and her eyes. Perhaps she would be athletic, like Petar, *and* write poetry. As a child, she would have worn pale blue frocks with embroidery. Oh no, they probably wouldn't wear embroidery in the country.

They passed a house that had been hit by a mortar, a corner of the second story crumbling. Since her daughter lived in the country, she would garden, tend to animals, perhaps; Ana hoped she grew roses as well as vegetables. In the evenings, she would tell her mother, a kindly, loving mother, but smart, too, well-read, steering her in all sorts of interesting intellectual directions, she would tell her mother about her troubles at school, and the mother would console her, extricate the lesson learned. The girl would trot off to do her homework, perhaps painting a delicate watercolor before bedtime. Rose and lavender.

"Your turn."

Ana had forgotten Bill. She felt alarmed, loath to confide, to feed the voyeurism.

"I had a wonderful grandmother. When she buttered a piece of bread, she buttered it all the way out to the corners."

"What does your husband do?"

"He's a writer." She thought about their conversation the night before. "Forbid" was not their language. She had no way of anticipating what his reaction to her departure would be.

"You?"

Why not. "A poet." Why was he bothering to give her a lift.

"How long have you been here?" she asked.

"Too long. Not that you don't have a lovely country."

"Why are you making this trip?"

"Scouting."

"For what?"

"Stuff."

"What kind of stuff?"

"Stuff that would interest my producer. He's a writer,

too, you'd like him. But on road trips you're better off with a techie. I can fix the car. How are you going to find your kid?"

She hadn't thought it through, afraid that if she thought about it she wouldn't come, that she would see the impossibility. She would be guided by instinct, records would appear, something would turn up, it was best not to ruminate. She hoped Emir was being attentive to Muhamed.

The road bent before three houses squatting on a slight incline in a clearing. Bill pulled off the road beside the narrow lane to the first house. "Going for information," he said. "Wait here."

Ana absorbed the slamming of the door as he left and watched him move toward the house. She studied the houses, which seemed undamaged. Stalactites hung from the eaves; smoke poured out of one of the chimneys.

She looked back at Bill, who was entering the first house. This was a good chance for her to ask some questions—he didn't have to know—and Ana slipped out of the car quickly, leaving the door slightly ajar so it wouldn't bang and headed toward the path of the house farthest away, at the edge of the woods, the one with the smoke coming out of the chimney. She stepped carefully through the patchy snow, alert for ice, walking past the forlorn garden to the left of the house. It began to snow again, and she pulled the knot in her scarf tighter as the wet flakes hit her face. Her previous sojourns into the Bosnian countryside had been idyllic forays into nature, her contact with villagers minimal.

She knocked on the front door, but didn't hear anything; she stomped her feet and looked around. The shutters were open. Snow was falling faster, and she knocked again, more loudly. When no one answered, she pushed the door gently, testing, and, as there was no resistance, opened it all the way. The small house appeared to be empty, and she stepped inside, seeking sanctuary from the snow.

Ana felt awkward, an uninvited guest, and would stay only a minute, not long enough for Bill to miss her. The fire blazed brightly—where were the occupants? Three places were set at the rough-hewn wood table, and food remained on the chipped plates, yogurt and some kind of beef perhaps, the knives and forks askew. Dishes lined the open cupboard. A painting of the Sarajevo skyline hung on the far wall, and framed photographs sat on a table next to a bottle of plum brandy. Ana became apprehensive that her intrusion might be misconstrued.

"Hello?" she called. When there was no response, she took tentative steps toward the other room, perhaps someone was ill? Ana walked into the bedroom, which was empty, and heard the front door of the house swing open with such force that it crashed against the wall. She turned abruptly, and reentered the first room, ready to greet her host.

❧

Anne heard the sirens of police cars speeding down the street; flashing red lights accompanied the screams.

❧

Marko, Petar's cousin, stood in the frame of the door, wind and snow whirling around him, holding a rifle.

Ana was relieved to see someone she knew. His cap pulled down almost to his eyes. He was stocky, his jaw square, his face weathered.

"I'm Ana Gusic!" Perhaps he didn't remember. She pulled her coat more tightly around her as the damp cold from the open door rushed through, and snow blew in on the wood-planked floor. "Petar's neighbor."

Marko looked around the room. "You live here now?"

"No."

He headed toward the bedroom. "Who else is here?"

"No one."

After glancing into the bedroom, Marko returned to the first room and looked at Ana, as if for the first time. He smiled.

Not a friendly smile. Ana's muscles tightened and she started walking slowly toward the door, still wide open, but Marko intercepted her and slammed it shut. He turned to face her. The smile.

"Where are your antiques now?" he said.

He motioned with his rifle. "In there."

Ana knew he meant the bedroom, but feigned confusion. She smiled as if they were at a tea party. "Do you remember? We met when you visited Petar."

"In there!" He shoved her with the rifle butt.

Dear God. Ana walked slowly into the bedroom. He probably just wanted her to check for something, or answer some questions, or stay in the room so she'd be safe. She screamed as she felt the butt of the rifle hit her between the shoulder blades. Marko pushed her facedown onto the bed. Ana tried to get up, but he had thrown himself on top of her; it felt like the weight of three men. Out of the corner of her eye, she saw him toss his rifle on the wooden floor. This isn't even my home, this is a mistake.

Marko brought her arms around to her back and held them down with the help of his knee, as she screamed. She tried to free herself, but he held her down, as if her head were being pushed over and over again beneath the ocean's swells. He reached around her neck and felt the knot of her scarf.

With surprising dexterity and precision he untangled the knot and pulled the scarf over her hair and across the back of her neck with exaggerated slowness, his hot breath on her skin.

"Hey!" Bill's voice. How long had he been watching?

Marko jumped off of her and grabbed his rifle. Ana turned over and sat up on the bed, as Bill and Marko eyed each other.

Marko glanced at the press credentials dangling from a chain around Bill's neck. He lowered his rifle and walked past Bill out the door.

Ana put her head in her hands. Bill came over and touched her hair, then quickly put his hand in his pocket. "Let's go."

She rose and Bill clasped a hand on her arm, half pulling her out of the house. The snow had intensified, and Ana felt exposed without her scarf, a vulnerability magnified to absurd proportions.

Flames rushed out of the other two houses, and Marko and three men with rifles had surrounded two unarmed men, one of whom was kneeling. The man standing was urinating on the head of the kneeling man, as Marko's friends jeered and laughed. Ana didn't want to see what came next.

She shivered so severely she could barely walk, and Bill pulled her along as she tried not to look at the men, tried to be invisible. Bill stared at them as he pushed her into the car, where she crumpled on the seat. He entered on his side and turned the vehicle around, heading back in the direction from which they'd come. He kept looking in the rearview mirror. At one point he stopped the car, adjusted the mirror, and pointed the lens of the video camera at the men and took some footage.

Ana didn't look back, didn't speak, ashamed she was willing to abandon her search, however temporarily, without protest, with such relief.

Bill looked over at her from time to time. "Better get your act together before we hit the checkpoint. It's no easy thing we're trying to pull off."

He was silent for a while, stopping occasionally to take photographs. Once he swung the camera around to include her, but she turned away.

"Does anyone else know you're making this trip?" he said.

"Just my husband."

The wind moaned in the pines.

She wished he wouldn't keep looking at her.

∞

Anne walked away from the stranger standing too close and moved to Craig's side; he introduced her to the man with him, a publisher. She asked the publisher something and let her mind drift as he provided a lengthy answer. Craig downed two slices of smoked salmon and started in on the caviar. The chunky silver bracelet he'd given her on their anniversary clanged against her glass. She'd left her pipe at home.

The man sipped his champagne. "Your husband told me about your novel." Another swallow.

Here it comes. Her heart tightened, the adrenaline surged.

"Why Bosnia?"

∞

The snow was tapering off by nightfall when Ana and Bill returned to Sarajevo, and the full moon lit up the profusion of tracks in the snow—bicycles, dogs, pedestrians. It was past curfew, and Bill kept his lights off as they drove through silent streets.

He moved past the sandbags, down the hill into the garage under the Holiday Inn. He had told her from the beginning that he wouldn't be able to drive her back to her building. Inside, they circled the garage slowly, passing a man getting something out of his trunk, and Bill pulled into a space at the far end of the garage, where the car jerked to an abrupt halt. He fumbled for something in the backseat, but Ana couldn't wait and opened her door. Although she still had the long walk home, she savored her relief as she fell out of the car. Breaking back into

Sarajevo was as dangerous as breaking out of it, and she couldn't believe the miracle of passing through the checkpoint without incident. She was bone tired, numb. How good the bed would feel. Muhamed and Emir. She slammed the door shut.

Before she realized he was out of the car, Bill was at her side, leading her by the arm. "This way." She thought the exit was in the other direction. Ana stumbled around in her half stupor through the dark garage, barely able to see. She lost her balance as Bill pushed her down on the concrete floor, and straddled her, pinning her arms to the ground; she was on her back.

"What are you doing!?" She screamed from the heart, loud enough for the other man in the garage to hear.

Bill smashed his fist into her face; she felt the sharp sting of an opening wound above her left eye. He put a hand over her mouth; she moved her head back and forth on the gravelly cement and tried to pry off his hand with her freed hand, buying precious time until the man came to her rescue. She wanted to bite Bill's hand, but he pressed too hard, sitting on her, holding her body immobilized between strong thighs. "You scream, I'll kill you."

Ana looked into his eyes, blood trickling down her face. She believed him.

He removed his hand from her mouth slowly, watching her. She didn't understand why the man they'd seen hadn't responded to her screams. Did he think it was a domestic conflict?

"Are you going to cooperate?" Bill said.

When she said nothing, he moved his hand to her

throat and tightened his grip. She grabbed his hand and jerked it away.

Yes.

A cat wailed.

∞

Anne's rape had occurred twenty-five years earlier, although she'd never told anyone. On Valentine's Day.

Just out of college (she'd received Emily Post and a strand of pearls at graduation), she'd moved into the city, into a new townhouse across the street from a public housing project. She lived in a group house, all female, but the group wasn't home; everyone had gone skiing over the long Presidents' Day weekend.

She'd just returned from a date with a new man, an Episcopal seminarian she'd met at church. "If you want to meet a nice man," her mother had said, "go to church." The minister had seemed very pleased to see her and apologized profusely for the unattractive homeless man who sat down on the pew beside her.

She'd had dinner at the seminarian's house. A sign in his den said, "If religion is a crutch, why is everyone falling down?"

When the nice man brought her home to her townhouse, he'd left the car running as he walked her to the door. It was snowing lightly.

"Hey man, your lights are on!" Hey man, your lights are on. That's what the rapist had said. Only they hadn't known he was a rapist. He was just a man walking down the street, probably returning from the late shift somewhere.

"Thanks, man!" the nice young man said. "I'll only be a minute."

Anne was a little nervous that he'd said that, but thought she was being paranoid. Nevertheless, "Why don't you come in for a few minutes," she said, wanting to wait for the stranger to pass. So the young man came in and they laughed *and talked for a while until she felt it was safe for him to go. After he left through the sliding glass doors to the garden, Anne locked the door, kicked off her shoes, and went to the kitchen for a snack, as was her postdate custom. She glanced at the clock as she opened the refrigerator door, which had tomatoes, peanut butter, and milk written on the list.*

She heard the sliding glass door opening, but knew it couldn't be the door because she'd locked it. She came out of the kitchen and saw him standing in the living room. In his twenties, jeans and a black jacket, about six foot two.

It was a bad situation. She would try talking with him. Anne couldn't remember what she'd said—asked him to please leave, probably. When she'd received her first obscene phone call, she'd said, "I beg your pardon?"

He looked around the room and down the corridor, wall-to-wall rose carpeting, floral upholstered furniture in a conversational grouping around a glass coffee table. "Who else is here?" he asked.

"My husband's upstairs."

He smirked, and moved toward her.

"He's coming home any minute."

He didn't stop.

She picked up a large umbrella (the symbolism didn't strike her until later) and started hitting him, screaming as loud as she could, trying to rouse neighbors from their beds at midnight. Ana knew the man next door could hear; the walls were paper thin, and she'd seen his light on when she'd come home. The woman on the other side would hear, too.

No one came.

The intruder grabbed the umbrella, pulled it out of her

hands, and started beating her with his fist, hitting her across her face and body. He pushed her down on the chintz sofa and got on top of her, still pounding her face. "Shut your motherfuckin' mouth or I'll kill you."

She stopped screaming. He stopped beating her.

Anne thought about Pavlov.

She'd read Manchild in the Promised Land *with fascination. Now she knew what motherfuckin' meant.*

His dark brown eyes were inches from hers. I could poke my finger in his eye. I'll kill you. A large pair of scissors lay on the table across the room. If she could somehow reach the table and scissors, stab him before he stabbed her. I'll kill you.

I'll do everything he says.

Get me out of this alive, God, and I'll never doubt again.

The man stood. "Get up."

He took her upstairs, past the gilt-edged mirror where a girl with a bloody, swollen eye stared back at her. "In here," he said. He led her into a pale blue bedroom with a brass bed. "Take off your clothes."

It's my fault. If I hadn't worn such a short dress.

Stay alive. Do everything he says. First the bloodstained blue wool dress, then the slip, bra, stockings, and underpants. He watched as she undressed. Everything he says. I'll kill you.

He looked at her naked body. "You're fat."

At five foot six, Anne weighed 110 pounds. It was confusing, humiliating.

It's my fault. If I hadn't had the glass of wine at dinner, I would have been more alert, clear thinking. I would have been able to persuade him to leave.

"*Lie down,*" *he said.*

Stay alive. She lay down on her back on the white, eyelet bedspread, knocking a stuffed dog to the floor. He unzipped his pants and lay down on top of her. He entered her.

She felt nothing.

Her face and body should hurt where he'd beaten her. She felt nothing, an all-encompassing numbness.

From a corner of the room, she watched a girl being raped.

She prayed it would end swiftly. He pumped and pumped. Nothing. There was no rising action. She didn't understand why the neighbors hadn't come in response to her screams; did they think it was a domestic conflict?

Anne's mother had taught her that it was improper to be alone with a man in an apartment without a chaperone.

"*Do you have a sister?*" *she asked.*

He didn't respond.

It's my fault. Anne had been raised not to have sex before marriage. *An eye for an eye.*

"*Turn over,*" *he said. Everything he said.* He entered her.

"*That's the wrong place,*" *she whimpered.* She felt like an idiot, a five-year-old, but that's what came out.

He pumped and pumped. There was no rising action. The cuckoo clock struck one.

This should hurt a lot. She felt nothing.

This is a very scary movie. I would like to change the channel.

"*Do you believe in God?*" *she asked.*

He pulled out of her.

"*I believe in God,*" *she said.*

Silence. No movement. She tried to think of the right thing to say.

But the moment lost its power over him, and he reentered her, pumped and pumped. No rising action.

"God wouldn't like this," the girl being raped said.

He pushed on and on. In. Out. In. Out. Her parents looked on from a silver frame.

"We're going downstairs," he said.

Lie down," he said, when they got to the sofa in the living room. He entered her. Pumped and pumped. She turned her face to the wall, papered with bluebirds pollinating pink flowers.

She had to accept that no one was coming to help.

It was her fault. Her ancestors had had slaves.

Anne was frantic for him to come so he would leave. He never did. It would go on and on. And then he would kill her. He would have to kill her because she had stared into his face and could identify him. He would be convicted and go to jail for a very long time; these were her thoughts; she was twenty-one.

She felt nothing. A single red rose, not fully opened, lay on the table; her date had given it to her since it was Valentine's Day. The book would have a single red rose on the cover and be called Valentine.

He pulled out of her and sat next to her. "Sit up," he said. He put her hand on his penis and rubbed up and down. He removed his hand. "Keep going!" he said. She moved her hand, pulling the skin up and down. Maybe this would work, maybe he would leave.

"Where did you learn that?" he said. Shame engulfed her.

"Come here," he said. He pulled her into the kitchen. The clock said she'd been raped for four hours so far. Her father had said he didn't believe in rape.

"Sit on the counter."

She must have misunderstood.

"The counter!"

Anne hoisted herself up and sat on the cold counter next to the paper towels. She thought about being fat.

He entered her. Anne felt nothing. If he ties me up or kills me, no one will find me for three days.

He never climaxed. Was that her fault, too?

"Get down," he said.

They went into the living room. "I'm going out of town," he said. "I need money."

"I can write you a check!"

He sneered. "Cash."

Anne opened her purse; two dollars peered out of her wallet.

He shook his head.

She ran into the kitchen and opened the beige canister where they kept the grocery money. "I need to buy a ticket for my wife, too!" he called out. Anne returned and handed him the money.

He counted it, then stuffed it into his wallet. "Will you pray for me?" he asked.

"Yes."

"Can I come back tomorrow night?"

"Yes."

"I have lots of friends in this neighborhood. If you ever tell anyone what happened, they'll kill you."

She promised.

He turned and walked out the sliding glass doors with rose curtains at either end. The snow beat against the panes; the garden was buried.

Anne turned off the light so she couldn't be seen from the outside. She sat down on the floor. He'd left the house, but that made no difference; he or his friends could come back anytime. There was no point in even locking the door, it hadn't kept him out before. She sat naked in the dark, too frightened to move, completely exposed, every day for the rest of her life.

10

Ana lay in the dark on the floor of the garage where Bill had left her, the back of her head pressed into the pebbled concrete. She fought the heavy urge to close her eyes.

She raised herself slowly, shaking, and pulled her clothes on. A warm stream of blood ran down her cheek from the burning wound above her eye, she licked the salty corner of her mouth. She pushed herself all the way up into a sitting position, her head throbbing. He'd gone, but he could come back.

If she'd listened to Emir, if she hadn't been so headstrong, so foolhardy. A woman on a trip with a strange man, in a war zone for God's sake.

She stood, bending over for a few seconds to allow her blood pressure to adjust, and leaned against a car momentarily to rest. When she was ready, she headed in the direction of what she thought was the exit. As she got closer and realized she was right, she allowed a sliver of hope. She glanced quickly behind and to either side, afraid to look too carefully, to locate terror in the shadows, and ran the last few steps to the exit and forced the door open.

A blast of bone-chilling air greeted her as she slipped into the Sarajevo night, wrapping her coat around her. The snow beat down on her, the wet, heavy kind that breaks the backs of trees. She turned left, toward home, away from the hotel, remembering the time a couple of weeks ago she'd joined the crowd at the Holiday Inn picking leftovers out of the trash.

No one was about; the snow fell silently, without witness, onto buckled roofs in the muffled city. She created footsteps where there were none, stopping frequently to look behind her, not knowing whether seeing someone would make her more, or less, frightened. She imagined Muhamed and Emir waiting. Surely Emir had not abandoned her? She put one frozen boot in front of another, her toes tingling in dampness, and shivered uncontrollably, teeth chattering. As long as Muhamed is all right. A dog snacked on a bloody lump covered with snow.

The moon hid in shame behind a cloud as she marched through empty streets past twisted lampposts, the whistling wind for companion. Towering shadows of buildings mocked as icy snow slid down the back of her neck under the collar of her coat, snow's heralded cleansing powers mere myth. She held her breath against her own stench, fighting the urge to tear off the filthy clothes, the ones the rapist had touched, the filthy skin. She fell into a pile of snow heaped by the side of the road and rolled in it.

It was her fault.

❧

It wasn't her fault.

Anne clutched the glass of milk and tucked her bare feet under her bathrobe on the nubby green sofa. Craig had fallen asleep immediately after they returned from the party.

The furniture threw shadows in the unlit living room, the red lights on the security panel like snake eyes. The radiator grieved.

Anne looked out the window at snow falling lightly on the empty, moonlit street. It was midnight. She contemplated the power of aftershave. The aroma lingering for years.

The phone grew larger, until it dwarfed everything else in the room.

It was ludicrous. Necessary.

She rose and walked across the cold, hardwood floor, tightening the sash of her white terry-cloth robe. She dialed. I'll kill you.

"I'm calling to report a rape."

"Anne Raynard."

"Yes."

"Twenty-five years ago."

❧

Ana slipped into the dark apartment quietly so as not to wake Emir and Muhamed, should they be there, and closed the door gently behind her, rubbing her index finger along the edge of the door to feel it even with the wall. She spun around, startled.

Emir didn't say anything.

She sank into the sofa. Emir went into the bathroom and returned with a damp cloth, which he dabbed at the cut above her left eye. She was glad Muhamed couldn't see her this way. He had begun wetting the bed.

"Something happened," she said to Emir. She opened her mouth, closed it.

"Do you know what happened?" He would have to name it.

He shook his head.

"We got out of Sarajevo, but didn't go very far." She stopped. "A place with some houses."

"Did something happen there?" he asked.

The prelude of Marko and his friends paled before the other. "Not there. Back at the garage, at the Holiday Inn." Couldn't he finish it.

"What?"

"Bill." Couldn't he see it, couldn't he say it.

"Bill?"

"The American photographer." She wiped her face with the back of her hand. She looked into Emir.

"Did he hit you?"

Ana glanced at the stove, the fire gone.

"He took my picture."

Emir folded the wash rag into a neat square, concealing blood.

❧

"What are you telling me?" Craig asked. He was still blinking in the glare of the overhead light. It had seemed to Anne when she woke him that the situation called for the starkest, brightest light, not a cozy bedside lamp.

The bedroom was spartan and neat; besides the antique dresser, which had belonged to her mother, only a bed and chair sat on the highly polished hardwood floor, a pink and gray oriental rug centered between the bed and the dresser. On the white walls she'd hung a large, rose-colored abstract painting in which the outline of a nude female was barely discernible, a brown-ink drawing of a man dancing, and a framed strip of blue, hand-embroidered Chinese silk populated with pagodas and men pulling rickshaws.

Craig lay on his side in the bed, supporting his raised head with an arm bent at the elbow, the black sheets hugging his form. When Anne had bought the sheets, the saleswoman had assumed she was buying them for a teenaged son or daughter. Margaret, her tail waving half-heartedly, was faithlessly curled up on the white comforter at Craig's abdomen, having abandoned Anne's side of the bed when Anne got up for milk.

"A man broke into the house where I lived," she said, "right after college."

"The one on Fourth Street?"

"By the public housing project."

"Was he a burglar?"

Anne glanced in the mirror above the dresser. It was an odd thing, how much better she looked when she'd been crying. The overwrought, reddened cheeks, the cleansed, glistening eyes. She peered out into the street through two slats of Levolor blinds. I'll kill you.

She looked back at her husband, a wonderful man who invested time when they made love. She'd never told him that too much time sent her spinning into flashback.

✺

Muhamed leaned his head back and drank his water. Emir rotated his tea cup ninety degrees to the left, then back to the right, then to the left again. Ana rose from the table to get more tea. They'd burned cookbooks for the morning fire; her mother-in-law had given them to her after her first dinner at Ana's house.

"Is everything all right?" Muhamed asked.

"Of course!" Ana and Emir said.

"I bet we've had our last snowfall of the season," Ana said.

"We always have a blizzard in March," Muhamed said.

Muhamed was right; spring wasn't coming.

"Where were you last night?" Muhamed said.

"I got caught in the snow."

"I guess you bumped into something."

"Exactly."

Muhamed ate donated American food, dried rations left

over from Vietnam, while studying Ana. He squinted at her, then opened his eyes wide. "You're all blurry."

Her heart stalled; the doctor had warned of vision problems. "Go to bed! Rest!" A ridiculous prescription, what else could she do.

Muhamed put his food down without disappointment and marched into the bedroom.

Emir was moving his tea cup back and forth. "I want you to know," he said, staring at the cup, "that I won't let what happened to you diminish my affection for you."

❧

"Are you sure you had locked the sliding glass door?" Craig asked.

Anne looked at him coldly. She understood the need to feel horrors are preventable or, at least, not random. How often she and Craig had discussed her father, how literal he was, the linear quality of his thinking, the paucity of metaphor. It made sense that her father would get Alzheimer's. Certainly it would never happen to them.

11

Ana thrust her hands into her coat pockets against the chill of the damp basement, determined not to miss a beat, to continue meeting the demands of daily life, to deprive the rapist of victory. It was actually kind of inspired, she thought, to look for fuel in the cellar—she planned to make soup for Muhamed. It wasn't because she was afraid to go out.

Emir had reported the rape to authorities, who had other things to think about, and he had begun lurking around the Holiday Inn.

Ana's eyes trained on the rough, uneven floor as she sought out abandoned items that could be burned, careful to watch for rats. The stimulus of the concrete floor made her dizzy, and she held onto a pole to steady herself.

The other tenants had pretty much picked the maze of

rooms clean; a couple of mattresses remained, along with the odd shoe or metal trunk. It was dark and difficult to concentrate, she worried about Muhamed. She thought she heard something and looked quickly behind her; nerves, an instrument strung too tight. She walked past a bicycle, cobweb-covered skis, and metal file cabinets, and turned into another room, jerking her hand away from the wooden doorway as a splinter pricked her finger. She spotted a flash of color in the corner of the room and stooped to pick up the red and blue toy soldier, rubbing her finger over the tin body. She heard a muffled cough.

Soundlessly, she looked around the room, but except for scattered objects on the floor, it was empty. The door to the built-in cedar closet was closed. Common sense told her to go upstairs, but she worried that someone might be hurt, a child perhaps.

"Damir?"

Whoever it was could be sick, perhaps he or she slept in the closet, or the door had locked behind him accidentally. She knocked on the door, without response. She opened it slowly and threw her hands to her face. Petar crouched in the corner.

He was almost unrecognizable, his hair and beard long and unkempt, his clothes torn and smeared, dark dirt under his fingernails; he'd lost a lot of weight. He didn't seem surprised to see her and evidenced no emotion, his eyes were glassy. She hadn't seen him since April; his apartment, two floors above theirs, was inhabited by refugees.

"What are you doing here?" she asked.

He looked at her as if he didn't see or recognize her.

"It's Ana," she said.

"I know." Even his voice was different, hoarse, weak.

"Are you by yourself?" he asked.

She nodded.

He stood slowly as if he were an old man, bones aching and joints creaking. Appearing to be in pain, he stepped out of the closet and looked around. He spotted one of the mattresses, sat down. "Food?"

She looked at the sunken cheeks, the hole in his boot.

"I won't go away," he said.

She climbed the wooden stairs. When she returned with bread, he was stretched out on the mattress, but sat up when he saw her. He devoured the bread, breaking it apart with dirty hands, picking up every crumb that fell on the dusty floor, rushing it into his mouth as if it might be snatched from him.

When he seemed to be finished, and had picked up each crumb from his lap and plopped it into his mouth, she began again. "Were you in Prague?"

He shook his head.

"Vienna?"

No.

"Where?"

He flicked something off of his trousers. Ana had never seen Petar like this; his hubris had evaporated with his flesh, and she wondered if he were dangerous, the sort of thing she didn't used to wonder about people.

"You'll keep it secret?" he asked.

What could he possibly tell her that anyone would care about? Who cares where he's been, who cares about anything but getting through the day. But she would promise as if it were life or death, because she needed something from him and wanted him in her debt.

"I deserted," he said.

She absorbed it. "Conditions must be awful in the army."

"It wasn't the Bosnian army."

A slow realization crept through her body like a blush, a possibility that was impossible.

She sat down on an edge of the mattress. "You've been shooting at us?"

"I didn't join for that, I joined because they said . . ." He grimaced, fell back on the mattress. A bread crumb sat on his beard.

The bullet that found Mira.

The world had gone mad; she would never recover.

They sat in silence as the dim light from the barred, single window grew fainter. A couple of drops of blood had stained the dingy, graying mattress, along with something else that could be urine.

The index finger had been severed from Petar's right hand, apparently an old wound that had now healed. "What happened to your finger?" she asked.

"An accident. I was a film projectionist; my finger got caught in the projector."

Petar had marched off to fight in a glorious war for God and country and ended up as a film projectionist.

"What kind of films?"

"Footage of rubble. They said Muslims bombed their own buildings so they could blame it on Serbs."

Did he believe that crap? She glanced down at the phantom finger on a hand that could no longer form the three-fingered Serb salute and looked back up at Petar, who had never been accident prone.

❧

The basement had grown darker, colder. A fat rat scampered across the floor.

Ana clasped her hands firmly together on the lap of her gray coat and sat erectly. "I need something from you. In exchange for silence." She let the words register.

"Where is our baby?" She had to remind herself that the child wasn't a baby anymore; it had been eighteen years.

"You never asked before."

"Would you have told me?"

He studied the mattress.

"Giving up the baby was very difficult for me," he said.

She tried to contain the rage.

"I took the baby to live with my relatives in the country. I wanted to be sure the child would thrive."

Good, that was good. He must have checked up. "Was it a girl?"

"A boy."

A boy! But she rather liked the idea. He and Muhamed could be friends.

"Does he know I'm his mother?"

"No."

"Does he know his mother loved him? That she didn't want to give him up?"

He looked in the far corner of the room.

"What color hair?"

"Blond."

"Eyes?"

"Brown."

"Where is he?"

Petar glanced at the stairs. She threw herself at him and shook him like a rag doll.

He pulled away and retied his boots. "Marko isn't my cousin," he said.

She tried to decipher his meaning.

"So?"

He turned toward the barred window.

She thought about Marko lying down with his full weight on top of her, his breath on her neck, the stink of brandy.

She added vomit to the stains on the mattress.

∞

Bright pink flowers burst from the pale blue background of the cardboard Kleenex box. The tuft of Kleenex erupting from the top sat up pertly, invitingly.

Anne was pleased with her rendition of the rape; she had included all of the details, added possible interpretation, symbolism, knitting meaning out of threads—everything presented professionally, factually, without the muddying fog of emotion.

She looked up at the white-haired, horn-rimmed psychiatrist making notes with a Mont Blanc pen on a yellow legal pad. He was a psychoanalyst, but this was her first visit, so she was allowed to face him. His black-suited bottom pressed firmly into the black leather chair. His credentials hung over the mahogany desk, and Anne squinted, trying to read the schools, not sure what the good ones were anyway. The room was lined with bookshelves full of leather-bound books used for reference, not reading.

The psychoanalyst looked over his glasses at her across the wide gulf of the rosy oriental rug like the one that used to be in her father's study. "You seem to have processed that experience well," he said. "Are there other issues we should discuss?"

Anne was flabbergasted; how could he be so stupid as to have bought into her act? She'd read about "pseudo-recovery."

She searched her life for acceptable material. "I started having anxiety attacks, shortly after the rape." She had tried so hard not to miss a beat, to continue meeting the demands of daily life, to deprive the rapist of victory. She hadn't lost a day of work, hadn't discussed it with anyone, hadn't wallowed; when her dog had been run over and killed by a car when she was a girl, she'd been required to take her piano lesson anyway. About a week after the rape, she'd walked past a group of construction workers who said things; she'd started shaking and hadn't stopped in twenty-five years.

"Anxiety attacks!" the psychiatrist said lustily. "That's something we should explore." He flipped through his black leather appointment book hungrily. Blinds at the window filtered out light.

∞

Ana lay in the darkened room on Muhamed's bed, with her arms pulled tightly around him as he slept; he fidgeted, and she loosened her grip a little. As he snored, Ana examined cracks in the white plaster ceiling, trying to determine which had preceded the war, which were new.

She tried not to think about Marko, particularly not to think of him as her son, which shot waves of nausea rolling through her. Marko's eyes were almond shaped, heavy lidded, like hers. It was impossible that a son of hers . . . . Are they really finding out that genes are more important than environment? And if environment shapes character, what were the implications for her own behavior if she'd been raised in Marko's circumstances?

She would not make excuses for Marko and his friends. Marko merged with Bill; they were animals, dark, foaming, pawing, muttering animals possessed by fiendish forces that had always and would always roam the earth like ravaging, howling dogs.

Muhamed was her only child. Light, life, reason. He coughed in her arms, his tiny body shaking like that of an old man caught in a death rattle.

We cannot protect our children.

∽

A green and purple marbleized design decorated the Kleenex box, an odd choice for a Kleenex box. The sheet emerging from the opening at the top of the box was limp, tired.

A week had passed since Anne's meeting with the Mont Blanc psychoanalyst; she'd moved on to the second name on her referral list. As she sat in the waiting room, she worried about the fact that she'd turned the American television cameraman in Sarajevo into a rapist. It was television camera-

men, after all, risking their lives, who had brought Ana's image to her in the first place; they had sounded the call to action.

The balding, bearded psychologist sat back comfortably in the soft, contemporary chair as he looked at Anne across the orange, whirlpooled rug; the fronds of palm behind him threw dappled sunlight on the wall. His undershirt peered out between two buttons of his coffee-stained shirt. A framed copy of a bad poem about the nightmare of childhood hung on the wall beside the cheery yellow couch where Anne sat. Sofa sections, chairs, and pillows formed a circle around the walls of the large room; a brown teddy bear with a red ribbon tied around its neck had been tossed casually in a corner, under a Ben Shahn print. The heater groaned.

The psychologist wore soft shoes resembling bedroom slippers, and his pudgy face dimpled when he smiled reassuringly at her. "Was it a serious rape?"

12

"I'm going to the front tomorrow," Emir said. "I've been ordered to dig trenches."

The men defending Sarajevo came home almost every night, but those digging trenches were closest to the snipers.

"They're rounding up everyone. Goran and Zlatko are going, too." He was tossing books into the fire in the stove, not checking titles. They had already chopped and burned the kitchen cabinets.

Ana sat down on the sofa and pressed her forehead into her hands; she'd been sweeping up broken glass—a jar and a bottle—from the morning's shelling. She hadn't told him about Marko and never would. Marko didn't exist. Only Muhamed.

"I should have done something long before this," Emir said.

"You're not a soldier."

At least it would keep him away from the Holiday Inn.

He placed more books in the fire, flames rose.

He sat down. "I will not receive a response from America. There will be no letter."

Pleas to end the siege of Sarajevo ricocheted through mountains, whispered across oceans.

He continued putting books in the fire. She recognized Beckett.

He looked over at her. "Is that a mole on your neck?"

Ana placed her finger on the mole. "It's been there since you've known me," she said evenly.

❧

"You have a smudge of dirt or something on your cheek," Craig said to Anne, making brushing motions in the air as if to wipe it away. A crystal bell, which Anne's grandmother had used to call the help, sat on the shelf behind him.

Anne brought her hand to the brown mark on her face. "It's an age spot," she said. "It's been there for two years, you've seen it before." The antique dining-room chair on which she sat had been broken, the cracks repaired.

A man walked past the window.

The only thing that brought her solace was the knowledge that humans grew a completely new set of skin cells over the course of seven years. Nothing he had touched remained.

❧

Three days after Emir began digging trenches, Ana heard knocking on the door. She put her hand to her chest and involuntarily held her breath. She had these sensations often now—sprinting heart, damp palms, quaking, a black lens on the world—and was afraid to leave the house for fear the symptoms would overwhelm her on the street. She was taking valerian for her nerves, as Anne Frank had.

Senka and Olga stood in the hallway, clutching irregular scraps of wood covered with snow; the March blizzard Muhamed had foreseen had blown in the night before. The women were from the next building; Olga and Mira had been classmates. Senka pushed her armload toward Ana. "We have enough for a few days, we thought you might want this."

Ana grasped the wood hungrily, overjoyed at the unexpected gift, with no idea what had prompted it. Acts of generosity, or barbarism, were not uncommon, but why them, why now? She didn't have the energy for the mental pursuit and simply grinned thankfully as she put Senka's offering of wood in the corner of the room and came back for Olga's. She recognized a branch of beech, good, it burned slowly. If she could keep Muhamed warm, she could keep him alive.

"I'm so grateful." She put Olga's wood on top of Senka's and returned to the women. "I'm so grateful," she said again. She smiled at the unmoving women, what did they want?

My God, how rude she was. "Please, come in," she said. The women rushed in like a dog to its dinner, finding seats in the living room before Ana offered.

"Tea?"

She put water on the woodstove, feeling the women watching her. They didn't speak while Ana brought teacups and saucers from the floor of the dining room—they'd burned the china cupboard. She'd rubbed dirt inside her cup this morning to clean it.

Ana watched Senka and Olga eyeing the contents of the apartment, as if for clues. The wood-burning stove retained its place of honor in the center of the room, and the nubby green sofa was in fairly good condition, although a number of long black hairs hung from it; her hair was falling out by the handfuls. The cracked, pockmarked walls were bare (the paintings removed to the bathroom for safekeeping), and the deep red oriental rug that had belonged to her parents still covered the parquet floor, now dirty and scuffed. The piano and piano bench were shorter, the legs chopped off in a frenzy of inspiration that had seemed to guarantee the piano itself would not be burned. Emir had added birds to the silver birch trees he'd painted on the plywood covering the windows, tiny, forlorn blackbirds. Ana hadn't picked up the brass-topped Ottoman coffee table, which was on its side and angled. Muhamed had used it for a fort in a battle that had not gone well for the table; he himself was a survivor, she told herself hourly. The mirror in the foyer had sustained a hit, reflecting a shattered world, and one of the antique chairs remained, its mate devoured by flames the previous week. The shelves were gone, the surviving books stacked on the floor. Clay pots where plants once grew sat in the corner. There was a piece of paper taped to the doorway:

God has not forsaken me, and He never will.

Anne Frank

Ana brought tea to the women and sat down. She began to feel almost lighthearted at the prospect of visiting with her neighbors, a speck of dust for the hole created by Mira's death.

"How are you, dear?" Senka said.

"Fine."

"Is there anything we can do?" Olga said.

Why the sudden interest? "I'm sorry Salko had to go to the front," Ana said. Emir had talked with Olga's husband there the day before yesterday.

Senka cleared her throat. "Did it hurt?" she asked.

Senka practically salivated in her hunger for details. You'd think people would have too much else to worry about, to do. How curious that the instinct to pry and gape, to feed on others, had survived.

Ana glanced down at the stack of wood the women had brought. A scrap sticking out from the bottom said 1958–1992—the remnant of a cross from a grave.

She looked back up at Olga and Senka, for whom her rape was a movie.

∞

The Kleenex box was empty, its gray interior evident. The social worker, whose hair was palely frosted, wore a pearl gray sweater and skirt, with matching heels and stockings.

They had been discussing the numbed state in which Anne had experienced the rape, and the social worker had related her experience of cutting a finger and going to the walk-in clinic to attend to the bleeding. It wasn't until she'd taken all the necessary pragmatic steps and reached the safety of the clinic that she'd had a delayed emotional response to the severity and danger of her situation.

The social worker smiled broadly, pleased at her contribution.

∞

Anne had given up on being understood. She didn't want to join a group of rape survivors; she was frightened of hearing about other places and ways people could be raped, how frequently it happened.

She looked out the living-room window at the cat waiting for Margaret. A church across the street enabled Anne to keep up with bridal fashions; black bridesmaid dresses were all the rage.

Craig had been sitting in the rocking chair, watching her. "When I was in the pacification program in Vietnam," he said, "I wore black pajamas, like theirs."

He never talked about Vietnam.

Anne tried to imagine a six-foot-two, blond, twenty-four-year-old in black pajamas with the five-foot-two Vietnamese.

"I spent a lot of nights in unpacified hamlets."

His eyes were half closed.

"We were shelled every night."

He was ice, staring into the distance. "A couple of times

VC *wandered into the village and chatted with me. I knew they were going to kill me."* Rigid.

"Once I was out with some Vietnamese on the way to a village and decided to stop and see an elderly man I knew—he made terrific machetes and was making me one. I told my friends to go ahead, I'd join up with them, and headed down the path to the old man's hut, the way I'd done a thousand times. It was dense jungle, really tall palm and bamboo trees. Sometimes the mist is so thick the lower half of your body disappears. The mud on your boots so heavy.

"I heard a chamber click; Charlie was up a tree drawing a bead on me; I dove to the ground and shot at him with my M-16, but it jammed, and he fired. I thought I'd been hit in the face—my eyes were stinging to beat hell and full of mud, but he'd shot right in front of me, kicking up all kinds of dirt. I got up and started running, but rifle fire erupted all over the damn place—it was an ambush. I dropped to the ground again and started yelling at my friends—they were about 200 yards away—and told them to shoot just above ground level. I crawled for the canal behind me—they were on the other side. The canal had a log across it, and when I got there, I fell into the canal and hugged the log from underneath, hanging and swinging from it—I monkey crawled across, bullets zinging all around me. Blood filled the canal, so I knew I'd been hit, but I kept inching forward until I was too weak and collapsed; one of my friends ran in and dragged me the rest of the way. We spent the next two hours retreating, shooting and running, shooting and running. Five hours later we were able to call in a chopper and I was taken to a secure compound."

A funeral procession left the church.

"I'd been shot in the shoulder and leg. There was a new lieutenant, who tried to treat my leg; he had trouble ripping my pant leg open and used his bayonet, goring me in the calf." Craig laughed a dry cough. "We had punji sticks around the bunker, and eight geese—the geese made a racket if anyone approached, if there was danger.

"Before I came, they built schools out of cement and reinforcing bar, but the VC would blow them up and take the cement and reinforcing bar to make bunkers. I thought we should build schools out of palm leaves and logs, and told headquarters to stop sending the cement and reinforcing bar, but it had been budgeted, so they kept sending it. We dumped it in the canal and kept building schools out of palm. They used to bring teachers from major urban centers; I thought it would be better to train local teachers. The villagers loved it; I was King of the Delta."

Church bells rang discordantly.

"One night the VC tied a teacher to the doorway of the largest school and set it on fire.

"It was Thanh, the guy who'd dragged me out of the canal.

"The VC left a Zippo lighter there, the kind GIs used. They murdered the rest of the teachers. Saigon started paying attention, and Navy Seals and the CIA moved in. The CIA was assassinating VC and would ask me if people were VC. I'd say no, they wouldn't believe me, and the next thing I knew a grenade would have been thrown into a hut, blowing up a whole family.

"I put in a requisition for geese. A thousand geese. I used Form 3964."

She sank into a chair.

"They sent me home."

He shifted in his seat. "I brought three posters back with me—the VC were offering a reward for my ears."

The airless room spun.

"When I came home, I tried to talk about it." He sat up and looked at her, watching her carefully. "There are things you can't tell people. You end up lonelier than before."

He slumped back into his chair, gone again. "Bend with the bamboo."

13

"We have to move the troops," Anne's father said.

"Let me take this opportunity to wish you Happy Visit," he said. "We've had a little back-set here at the office. A little up-mix."

"I have more places than usual to sleep," he said. "I take naps on the Baltimore Orioles field. At first I thought it would be a problem. They like to play baseball more than anything, and I can understand that, I'm that way, too. I don't know what I'll do if they throw the ball to me; I have only fifty cents in my pocket. I'm so mixed up, I won't be much help. I'm trying to do so many things, and I can't do right, and I want to do well."

Anne's family had been making fun of her father for years before he was diagnosed. It was too late to apologize.

Anne asked her mother how she coped. "I try to remember how, when I married your father, everyone told me I got the prize. And I did, I got the prize." Her arms were black and blue where he held her.

Anne talked with Craig on the phone. "It was a good idea," she said. "The geese."

Her father's best friend had died. Anne removed his number from the telephone Speed Dial and fingered the paperweight on her father's cherry desk: "O God, thy sea is so great and my boat is so small." Her mother sat at her own desk forging her husband's signature on birthday cards for the grandchildren.

Anne stood abruptly and went to her parents' bathroom, which had a hand-painted "Bathroom" sign on the door with a drawing of a toilet. She pushed the stack of diapers and her mother's heart medicine aside to reach the Kleenex.

She spoke in hushed tones with her mother about her father's move to a nursing home.

"What did you say?" he asked. He sat at the dining-room table wearing a body-length bib. The oriental rug under his chair was covered with plastic.

It was raining nonstop.

❈

Anne lay on a sleeping bag on the floor next to her father's bed on his first night in the Alzheimer's ward. She'd made a nuisance of herself all day accosting people in the hall, *shrieking about her father's likes and dislikes. The history channel, tapioca pudding, the Orioles, car keys in his pocket. Mashed potatoes because they were "flexible." Vanilla ice cream with chocolate sauce, holding hands.*

A tall, elderly man with a large, shiny forehead pushed the door open.

"I'm sorry, this isn't your room," Anne said.

"Yes it is! I own all the rooms on this floor and the floor above!"

A pink-uniformed female aide took him out.

Anne listened to her father thrashing about, his knees bent on the short bed, the "Do Not Resuscitate" bracelet banging against the headboard.

"Where is the one who ordinarily sleeps with me?" he asked.

∾

Anne sat next to her father at the Sing-Along with Jerry. Jerry wore a blue cardigan sweater and had gray hair and large black glasses. He played the piano in the center of the Common Room, which had wallpaper of a beautiful meadow at sunset. The attendants were enthusiastic.

Anne studied the well-worn songbook. Most of the songs were Irish, and she'd never realized how sad they were. She tried to sing.

An attractive, high-cheekboned woman across the room sat silently, head tilted up with a haughty expression that had outlived its appropriateness, watching the proceedings with alarm. A woman in a wheelchair started screaming. A woman in a soft, baby blue bathrobe with matching bedroom slippers turned to the woman in the wheelchair and shouted, "Oh, shut up!"

Jerry played "The Star-Spangled Banner," and Anne's father struggled to stand, but couldn't. Anne looked at the scar on her father's left cheek where the Japanese bullet had emerged. "Do you remember World War II?" she'd asked him yesterday. "Of course." "What do you remember?" "Horrible." Why wasn't everyone screaming.

The woman in the baby blue bathrobe sang vigorously off-key. Anne broke the large cookie into small pieces and handed them to her toothless father one by one. He wore the red plastic lei he'd been given and struggled with the red plastic hat, which didn't fit. He sang "Edelweiss."

A couple of people were dancing. Anne turned to her father suddenly. "Would you like to dance?"

"Okay," he said, which could have meant, "The sun is out," or, "I have an itch on my left calf."

She helped him to his feet and was pleased that he remembered where to put his hands. They leaned to the right, then to the left. Her father moved precisely on beat, which thrilled her beyond measure. She brushed a cookie crumb from his beige cardigan sweater and tried to pull a protective psychological shield around them: I'll never see these people again, who cares what they think. She rocked in her father's arms, the peace of a newborn sucking at the breast.

Her father looked over her shoulder, scanning the room for more interesting partners.

❧

Anne and her father returned from their walk, and she shook rain from the umbrella and removed his yellow slicker. She took her pass to the Alzheimer's ward out of her purse as they approached the entrance, where two faces pressed against the glass window of the door from the other side, women waiting for opportunity. Anne slowed down, hoping the women would leave. They knew what they were doing.

Anne positioned her father at the door and instructed him. "The minute I say 'go,' push on the door and enter as fast as you can. I'll be right behind you." He nodded.

Anne slipped her pass over the electric eye, shouted, "Go!" and shoved her father through the door with her right hand, while holding up her left arm to fend off the women who were trying to push out from the other side. Her father, ever the gentleman, held the door open for the escaping ladies.

One of the women who camped out at the exit was the woman in the wheelchair who'd screamed at the Sing-Along. She had hazel eyes, like Anne's, and the same wide jaw, hair held back and up with a barrette. There were more wrinkles and sags, more white in her hair. The woman had spotted Anne's pass and rolled silently behind her wherever she went, stopping when Anne stopped, starting up again when Anne moved.

Anne and her father returned to his room, where Mr. Danovitch slept in her father's bed. Anne woke him and took him out.

She cleaned up the bathroom floor.

"I'm sorry," her father said.

He grasped her arm and looked her in the eye. "There's a man here who's cruel to me and the others."

I cannot protect this child. Anymore than he could have protected me. She would forgive her father, if not the rapist. If not God.

Old people make things up. Besides, all of the attendants are female.

She fingered the pass in her pocket.

She put on a videotape of her brother's young children; her father waved at them. They watched a tape of his eightieth birthday party. "Who's that?" he asked, pointing at himself. The wheelchair squeaked in the hallway.

Her father's history books, none of them written after 1960, filled the bookshelves under a small painting of blue forget-me-nots. His wedding picture stood on the dresser, along with a "Get Well Soon!" card from his five-year-old granddaughter; other family members populated the top of the shelf and the windowsill. The Papa chair had survived the move from her parents' apartment, as had the enlarged, de-tailed, framed map of Alabama hanging above the bed; a stuffed dog wearing an Orioles baseball cap slept on his pillow. His prayer book and Bible rested on the bedside table, and someone had underlined: "Take therefore no thought for the morrow: for the morrow shall take thought for the things of itself. Sufficient unto the day is the evil thereof."

"Air strikes ruled out in Bosnia," her father said, staring at the newspaper by Anne's purse.

"Do you know who I am?" she asked.

His face contorted with the terrible struggle of trying to

pass another test he was doomed to fail. A translucent, tear-shaped drop of maple syrup hung from his blue cotton shirt.

"Are we related?" *she said helpfully.*

"Certainly not!"

Anne kissed him on the forehead and released his hand. She turned to gather her things.

"You're not coming back, are you?" *he said.*

The night shift was coming on; a male attendant appeared. Anne nodded at the large, sullen man, and held the door open for him.

The building was airtight. You couldn't open a window, or hear the rain.

14

Anne sat in the Quaker meeting house feeling wrong. The feeling had begun when she'd called to ask what time they had services at the church. "Meetings at the meeting house," she'd been informed.

The visit with her father had infused her with urgency, and she'd rushed to get to the building on time, practically knocking people down on the sidewalk as she passed, forcing one little boy into the gutter. Now she watched the same people ambling into the room casually, slowly, on time after all, as she sat on the bench panting. She swung her crossed leg rapidly.

She was dressed wrong. She'd hastily put on her uniform for "slightly dressy"—black velvet slacks, black boots with two-inch heels, one of her three black chenille sweaters. Shiny silver earrings glittered between brown strands, silver bracelets *on her wrist. She'd grabbed the first lipstick in the drawer and applied what she now realized was a garish purple, Episcopal purple.*

As the congregation, or whatever they were called, walked into the spare, altarless room, they looked almost Amish—some wore suspenders over workshirts—as if they'd wandered down from the mountains. Many men had beards, women were without makeup, clothes were simple, un-adorned. Anne felt like a cheap Christmas-tree ornament.

The members smiled pleasantly, with inner confidence she thought, not in performance, as they found seats in the quiet room. No stained-glass windows, no decoration or arti-fice, only a working fireplace centered in a white space with plain wooden benches (they probably wouldn't call them pews), the occasional crackling or resettling of burning wood the only music. She never thought she'd miss an organ.

The room filled, and then someone closed the double wooden doors, trapping the silence inside. No one spoke or moved. She had an overwhelming urge to cough, laugh, spit, cry, scream, and go to the bathroom. She was eight years old, in the school library, and the list of prohibitions was intoler-able. How did they stand it? She surveyed the pacific crowd.

Deep breaths, she would try deep breaths. Calm, she re-peated to herself, calm, imagining CALM in large black let-ters, then short, wavy, fuzzy ones, then giving up on calm altogether and focusing on "float" instead. She looked around again; why didn't someone say something, or sing something? Where was the ceremony, the message? The wait-ing was unbearable. She'd neglected breakfast, and her stom-ach whined.

Was this it? Was this what they came for? She looked out the window at sunshine, freedom. Craig had been raised as a Baptist and taught Sunday School as a teenager, but had been fired when he took the class outside and told them God was in the sky and trees. Anne saw an unleashed dog waiting on the sidewalk by the meeting house, a menacing sight in a town of rigidly enforced leash laws. Quaker dogs probably don't need leashes.

She plunged into prayer; surely that was the unannounced agenda. She prayed for her mother and father, for Craig, for the Vietnamese. She prayed for her son, and for Margaret. She prayed for Ana. Praying for herself seemed self-indulgent.

She'd been church-shopping sporadically for twenty-five years, a journey rife with unfulfilled longing. Frequently it was architecture that disappointed, or an uninspired minister, lack of interior light, parishioners that included no one she wished to befriend, a lengthy commute, gaudy stained-glass windows, an overwhelming boredom with the proceedings. Sometimes monklike chanting disturbed, other venues provided suitable intellectual fodder and democracy, but lacked God. She had selected the Quaker church for experimentation because of its proximity to her house.

While she knew the impediments she raised to religion were silly, she still stumbled over the larger one—reason. But some things were more persuasive than reason. There were religious temperaments, she believed, and she had one—a heightened receptivity to all things spiritual, or faux spiritual. She'd been conversing with the dead for as long as she could remember and would feel their consoling presence when

needed; she didn't believe this was a function of her imagi-
nation. Reason wouldn't take her where she needed to go
and was itself, she'd been told, historically and culturally
specific.

She returned to her surroundings and realized that she'd
calmed down, the buzz of voices stripped away, the silence
no longer threatening. She would send no noisy prayers
hurtling skyward. She would receive.

∞

Emir placed the Koran in Ana's hand. "The mujahideen
gave it to me," he said.

She imagined the swarthy, turbaned men—Iranians,
Arabs, Turks, and Pakistanis—and their veiled women
dressed in absurd black robes. The book could be used for
fuel.

Ana opened it at random: "It was He who sent the two
seas rolling, the one sweet and fresh, the other salt and bitter." She hurled the book onto the stack of wood in the
corner.

"They gave me something else," Emir said. He set a
brown-paper parcel on the coffee table and opened it, revealing a syringe and bottle of liquid.

Dear God.

"He showed me how to do it."

Emir and Ana ran into Muhamed's room, where Muhamed was building a bridge between two piles of books
with cards.

Emir put up his fists as if to box with him. "We should
wash his leg."

Ana went to the bathroom and returned with a blue washcloth, sitting down on the bed next to Muhamed. "Upper thigh," Emir said.

Ana rubbed the damp, soaped cloth on Muhamed's thigh and left to wash the cloth out, returning to rinse the soap off his leg before drying it with his blue towel. She put her arm around him; Emir sat on the other side.

Emir rolled the bottle between the palms of his hands. He opened the alcohol wipe they'd given him and passed it across the top of the bottle's rubber tip. Ana watched Muhamed watching Emir. She hoped Emir knew what he was doing. He raised the syringe and pulled the plunger out at the bottom until it reached the appropriate measure, then pressed the needle at the top of the syringe down through the top of the bottle and forced the plunger down. The needle was fat and long. Keeping the needle in the bottle, he turned the bottle upside down and jerked the plunger halfway to the mark on the syringe; he pressed it in again. What if he spilled. He pulled the plunger out to the correct indicator and removed the needle from the bottle.

He opened another alcohol wipe and cleaned a spot on Muhamed's thigh, pinched the skin, and inserted the needle into it, like a dart onto its target, pressing the plunger down, the insulin in. Ana jumped; Muhamed didn't flinch. Emir let go of the skin and pulled the needle out, pressing the alcohol swab to the puncture. Ana memorized the steps to life.

It would require time to take effect, but Ana and Emir sat quietly, waiting, watching. There was the danger of reaction.

Muhamed looked from one to the other. "I think we should change the ending of Anne Frank."

Ana shot a glance at Emir. "Okay."

"I'll go first," Muhamed said. "I think she survived the war and got to go to university and study mathematics." He looked at Ana. "Now you."

"At university, she met and fell in love with the most charming man, a man who danced with the stars. She married him, and they had a child, a wonderful son, whom they named Otto, after Anne's father. And late at night, after Otto was tucked safely in bed and sound asleep, Anne would write poetry." She turned to Emir.

"And her husband loved her with a ferocity that young girls writing diaries can't even imagine."

❧

Gripping the end of the clean, sweet-smelling black sheet, Anne flung it high into the air before laying it down on the guest-room bed. She tucked in all four corners, throwing the cover sheet down on top of the first, being careful not to get it tangled with the bamboo plant in the corner. She smoothed wrinkles.

Anne stuck a hand in her jeans pocket and pulled out a strip of paper that said Inspector #10. Last night she'd dreamt she was being chased again. She killed him.

She opened the closet and removed the collapsible mahogany luggage rack and set it under the framed photograph of her one-year-old grandfather wearing a dress. She'd received a comforting visit from her grandfather last week,

190

on the twenty-second anniversary of his death, and was grateful to whomever or whatever arranged for, or permitted, such events.

She pulled black guest towels and washcloths from the linen closet and placed them on the bed. They'd been bought new for the last guest and had deposited hundreds of tiny black blobs all over her body; Anne hoped the towels had aged sufficiently. Instructions for the radiator lay on top of the bookshelf—turn knob to the left to open, all the way to the right to close. She stroked her manuscript, which kept her company, and set it on one of the shelves. She closed the blinds on the window facing the neighbors and opened those on the backyard.

The drifts of snow were beginning to shrink in a silent, mysterious process that she thought should be accompanied by loud groans and shrieks. Tall, mature trees lined the perimeter of the yard; birches bent low to the ground, beaten down by winter. Last night a racoon the size of a small pony ran across the circular patio with its missing and broken bricks. Soon, single red and yellow tulips would pop up in the lush green ivy. The pear tree produced fruit every other year; how could it remember. A branch of the weeping cherry tree had broken off. The tree, her favorite, was always the first to bloom, and Anne watched, and waited, for pale pink blossoms that died within a week.

We know God exists because we miss him.

15

The blade penetration is slight, loosening only a few clods of dirt, like frozen mud pies, which Ana lifts and swings to the side. She drops the shovel to the ground and stoops, brushing the fresh snow away from the spot where she digs. Her mittens have holes in them, and she feels the cold on her naked flesh as her hand sweeps the white cover. The lightly falling snow slides down her cheeks like a baby's tears, and she stands and straightens herself, placing a hand at the small of her back, which aches slightly. The dark shadow of a gravestone falls on the new snow.

There's a lull in the fighting; boundaries have been rearranged. She's digging up her mother's grave, which now lies in Serb territory; she'll move her to Muslim soil. Before the war, her Muslim ancestry formed no part of her identity.

Men with a cart are coming to complete the job and arrange for transport. Emir had wanted to come, but she'd asked him to watch Muhamed. The bleakness of her task is offset—Muhamed's return to health, the ebbing of hostilities—and now they've received word that they have a sponsor, a woman in Massachusetts, and Ana, Emir, and Muhamed will live with her in a town called Cambridge. Petar can have their apartment. It's painful, the leaving, but she has to think of Muhamed. She sinks the blade in.

It's late afternoon when she begins the walk home, and the snow has stopped. Dusk is considered a sad time, but she's focused on the positive, on the future. Her nervousness has diminished, and she's pleased that she can walk the streets without threat of real or imagined danger.

People mill about as if at a carnival, and she thinks she sees tufts of new, green grass. She walks past a playground—seesaws, slides, a merry-go-round, broken, red roof tiles. She's saved enough water to have a real bath tonight, not a sponge bath. It's windy, cloudy. A front is moving in; they sit on the cusp between seasons.

It's growing dark, and she quickens her pace, stepping over a dead bird, discarded clothing; her jeans snag and rip on a jagged chunk of concrete. She thinks she hears a rifle crack, but it must be construction; people are daring to rebuild. There's another one, no mistaking it, and another. She moves to the inside of the sidewalk, pressing against protective buildings, tall, bloodied buildings ripped and torn, as she'd done countless times before. Balconies droop, paint and plaster peel. Surely Emir heard the first shots and took precautions; he'd removed the plywood protecting the windows from snipers when the ceasefire began. Muhamed reads at the window.

She turns the corner onto her street, strewn with bits of masonry, and picks up speed, leaping over garbage. It's damp, cold, and the road is pocked with craters, puddles, a bloodied rug. The smell of sewage, a broken doll. Mud mixes with snow; tracks cross over one another, trampling. Ana begins to run, balling her fist against bullets, which now come faster.

PERRIN IRELAND has worked as a filmmaker and as Associate Director for Drama and Arts at the Corporation for Public Broadcasting and as a senior program officer at the National Endowment for the Arts. She lives with her husband in Cambridge, Massachusetts.

This book was designed by Donna Burch. It is set in Legacy type by Stanton Publication Services, Inc., and manufactured by Maple Vail Book Manufacturing on acid-free paper.

Other Graywolf titles you might enjoy are:

Salvation and Other Disasters and *Yolk*
by Josip Novakovich

Night Talk
by Elizabeth Cox

How the Body Prays
by Peter Weltner

Jack and Rochelle: A Holocaust Story of Love and Resistance
by Jack and Rochelle Sutin, edited by Lawrence Sutin

Nola: A Memoir of Faith, Art, and Madness
by Robin Hemley

Central Square
by George Packer